Discovering Mr. Darcy

Discovering Mr. Darcy

LEENIE BROWN

LEENIE B BOOKS
HALIFAX

Contents

Dear Reader,

This novella is part of my *Dash of Darcy and Companions Collection*. These *Pride and Prejudice* inspired stories are quick, sweet reads designed to fit perfectly into a busy life.

Dash of Darcy titles in this collection will focus on Darcy and Elizabeth, while each *Companion Story* will focus on characters from *Pride and Prejudice* other than Darcy and Elizabeth and will be a sequel to a *Dash of Darcy* story.

The books in this collection are numbered in the order in which they were published and contain a complete HEA (happily ever after) for the hero and heroine. However, you may wish to know that all *Companion Stories* will reference events in the *Dash of Darcy* story to which they are a sequel, so reading those stories together will provide the greatest enjoyment.

Thank you for selecting to spend time with this

story. It is my desire that you will find a sweet escape within its pages.

Happy Reading!

Leenie B.

Chapter 1

"Fitzwilliam," Lady Catherine called to her nephew, Colonel Richard Fitzwilliam, as he passed the door to her sitting room. "Your call can wait," she said in answer to the reply she knew was coming.

Richard sighed and turned into the room.

"Just Fitzwilliam." Lady Catherine's tone was stern as she looked down her nose and made a brushing motion with her hand, indicating that her other nephew, Fitzwilliam Darcy, should leave the room. "Close the door," she called after him. She waited until it was latched and she heard footsteps moving away from the room. Then, she took Richard by the arm and pulled him further into the room.

"Sit." She motioned to a golden tufted chair on

the edge of a grouping in front of a window that looked out onto the front garden of the house.

Richard rolled his eyes and did as instructed. It was pointless to do otherwise. Lady Catherine always had her way, or there was a price to pay. It was far cheaper and easier to just listen. "To what might I ascribe the honor of this private conference?" It was likely some matter regarding the groves that she wished him to see to during his stay, for a stay at Rosings was rarely one of pure leisure.

Lady Catherine's eyes narrowed at his cheeky tone, but she did not reprimand him for it. He was always attempting to stir her ire, but today, she would allow no such distractions. She stood near the window and tilted her head to peer out and around toward the door where Darcy was just exiting. "It is time he marries," she said.

"Darcy?" Richard's eyes grew wide in surprise. This was not the conversation he had expected. In fact, it was a conversation he had always wished to avoid — at least with his aunt, that is.

She nodded, and leaving her vantage point at the window, she took a seat across from her nephew. "Yes, Darcy. Georgiana is not getting any younger and will need someone besides just her brother to guide her through her first season."

"But Anne –" Richard began. He knew neither Darcy nor his cousin Anne wished to marry the other, and he was prepared to argue their points.

"Not Anne," Lady Catherine interrupted. "They would not suit."

"Pardon?" Richard was at a loss for words. His aunt had always insisted that Darcy would marry Anne. In fact, it was a supposed engagement that had kept Darcy from feeling a need to begin looking in earnest for a lady to help him secure his estate for future generations.

Lady Catherine picked at a small flower on the arm of her chair as she avoided meeting his eyes. The supposed engagement to her daughter had been merely an elaborate ruse to prevent a most disastrous outcome for Darcy. "He was not ready to begin a family. I had to keep him from rushing forward into doing his duty somehow."

Richard's mouth dropped open and then snapped shut. There were still no coherent thoughts forming in his mind. What his aunt was currently saying was clashing with what she had always said previously. Had she not taunted Darcy about doing his duty by marrying Anne?

She shook her head as if reading his thoughts. "Darcy was never going to marry Anne, and Anne knew it."

Richard's brows furrowed, and his lips pursed into a perplexed scowl. "You will need to explain."

Lady Catherine rose and walked to the window. Darcy was still pacing in the front garden. She watched him take six long strides away and then back. One foot fell in front of the other in perfect time and in equal measure. It was very much who he was — proper, dignified, well-ordered. "I promised his mother that I would see him marry well and for love." She raised a brow at Richard, causing his mouth to snap shut on whatever exclamation of surprise he was about to utter. "When Darcy's father died, Darcy was not ready to take on the responsibilities of an estate and make a proper decision about a wife. He would have rushed pell-mell into an untenable marriage that would have perhaps resulted in a family, but not a happy one. He would have sat down, drawn up some supposed list of qualifications of a proper wife, and gone about the business as if he were hiring a maid — without one thought about the misery he would face as a result of his calculated methods." She tipped her head and gave Richard a firm look. "Do not tell me he would not have done so. You know as well as I that he puts duty before everything." She shook her head. "I still think he has no idea what sort of wife he requires."

Richard laughed. This conversation was not at all what he had dreaded it would be. In fact, it was proving to be rather entertaining. "And you do know what sort of wife he requires?"

Lady Catherine returned to her chair. "I do, and I have found her." She chuckled at the way Richard's mouth dropped open again. "What Darcy needs is a simple country miss with a keen mind."

"And you found her?" Richard asked incredulously. His aunt did not travel, and so far as he knew, there were no acceptable country misses who frequented Rosings.

Lady Catherine raised one shoulder and let it drop slightly. "I believe I have." She leaned forward as she prepared to tell him how she had done it. "My parson is the heir to an estate that is entailed — a distant cousin or some such thing. It is difficult at times to follow his meandering."

Richard raised a brow and smirked, earning a rap on the knee.

"I am not meandering."

Richard inclined his head in acceptance although the smirk did not fade from his lips.

"Anyway, this cousin has five daughters — three of a good marriageable age and two just reaching it." She smiled as the smirk dropped from Richard's face and was replaced with amazement. Five was a substantial number of daughters. It was not the largest she had heard of but substantial none the less. "I sent Mr. Collins to find a wife from among them because I reasoned that if he should marry one, then the others might be asked to visit on occasion, and I might be able to select one for Darcy."

Richard shook his head. "How did you know these ladies would be simple country misses with intelligence?"

Lady Catherine shrugged and shook her head. "There was no guarantee that they would be, but Collins had said their father eschewed town and spent the chief portion of his time in his study. I thought it likely that at least one daughter might have inherited her father's love of books and learning."

Richard nodded. That made sense. It was unlikely that all five daughters would be completely unlike their father. "Was Collins successful?"

Lady Catherine laughed. "No, he was not, and I really should have known he would go about it wrong. He tends to bungle things; however, in his bungling, he has made my task of selection most easy." She laughed again. "She refused him — soundly, and she is not taken with Darcy. Quite the contrary. She thinks him proud." Her eyes fairly danced with mirth. "Collins did secure a wife, however, and Mrs. Collins happens to be the future Mrs. Darcy's particular friend. That is how I know so much about my choice. Mrs. Collins is a lovely lady, very sensible — quite the opposite of her husband."

Richard's head tilted to the side as things began to come together into a coherent plan. "Your parson has a guest."

A smile split Lady Catherine's face. "Upon my urging, he does."

"And she is the lady you have selected?"

Lady Catherine's brows flicked upward quickly. "Clever, is it not?"

"Diabolical," Richard replied dryly.

Lady Catherine shook her head. "Did you see how quickly Darcy agreed to visit the parsonage? I assure you it is not because he has a fondness for my parson." She leaned forward again and spoke in a whisper. "He danced with her."

Richard blinked. "Darcy danced?" That did hold some weight then. Darcy did not dance with anyone outside of his close sphere of friends.

Lady Catherine gave a satisfied nod. "Danced and argued with her and then fled the area. He is smitten; mark my words." She rose and motioned for Richard to follow her. "Note how he acts on your call, and when they come for dinner this evening, flirt with her. You will see I am right."

Richard rested his hand on the door knob. "And if you are right, what then? If they have argued, it follows that one or both might not be willing to enter into a marriage."

"One does not have to be willing to enter a marriage for a marriage to happen," replied Lady Catherine with a sly grin.

"A compromise?" Richard could not help the small bit of excitement he felt about the possibility of a sneak attack.

"I shall not admit to it now or later," said Lady Catherine. "But they will marry. We shall see to it."

Richard chuckled as he left the room. While Darcy might have managed to outmaneuver the ladies and their mama's in the ton, he would stand no chance against their aunt.

~*~*~

"You are smiling," Darcy noted as Richard joined him in the front garden. Smiling after the completion of an interview with Lady Catherine was not a typical response. Rubbing your temples and seeking fresh air like a drowning man was a more likely response. Though Lady Catherine could be quite pleasant and even indulgent at times, she was more often than not demanding when she required an interview.

"It is a pleasant day, and I have escaped from our aunt with no more than a lecture on doing my duty while in residence." It was not entirely truthful, but there was enough truth in the statement for Richard to speak without so much as a pang of conscience. In fact, there was something rather like anticipation stirring in him as he considered how he and his aunt might capture their quarry. He would do as instructed and make his observations, and then, armed with the proper intelligence, he and Lady Catherine would contrive a plan.

"Yes, well, your duty only involves touring the grounds." Darcy knew his duty, as his aunt saw it, was to become the owner of the grounds through marrying her daughter, Anne. It was a duty that he in no way wished to fulfill. He sighed and rubbed his temple, thankful that he was out in the fresh air.

Richard glanced at his cousin. "You should tell her of your refusal to marry Anne."

Darcy drew in a deep breath and expelled it. "I intend to do so before we leave, but to do it now would make our stay more than a little unpleasant."

Richard's brows furrowed. "You truly mean to tell her?" He had told Darcy to speak to his aunt on each occasion when they journeyed to Rosings. Darcy had always claimed he would when the time was right. However, the correct time never seemed to present itself.

Darcy nodded. "It is time I consider marrying in earnest. I am nearly thirty, and Pemberley needs an heir. It is best to think of that while there is still hope of securing a wife happily." There was an heir to produce for Pemberley, this was true, but it was not his real reason for considering marriage. No, that reason, the lady he wished to find a way to marry, was currently installed at the parsonage in Hunsford. He had tried to escape it. He had hidden away and surrounded himself with work. He had attended functions and the theater. He had done everything he could think of to avoid what his heart was telling him because his heart's wishes did not match with the list of wifely qualifications in his head.

Richard chuckled. "You think that with an estate the size of Pemberley and the looks of your father, you would have to force a lady into marrying you even if you were twice your age?" He shook his head. "I cannot think of any lady of my acquaintance who would refuse you."

"I am not eloquent," Darcy replied. "Ladies find my reserve off-putting."

"That is not without remedy. You have no trouble smiling and talking with Bingley or me."

"Both you and Charles are like brothers. I have no trouble speaking to Georgiana, either."

Richard twirled his walking stick in the air and slashed at a bush along the path. "I have seen you speak to ladies at soirees."

"I have been terse and often stumble over my thoughts." Darcy caught a loose stone with his toe and sent it skittering across the path. "I wish it were not so, but it is."

"The right woman will loosen your tongue." Richard gave him a sidelong appraising look. There was a slump to Darcy's shoulders as if he had already given up hope of ever being able to speak to the right lady. "Have you found a lady?"

Darcy blinked. "N-no," he stammered, his ears heating with embarrassment. He was certain from the twitch of his cousin's lips that his reply was not accepted. Hopefully, Richard would just let it pass. "Bingley thought he had found a lady." Perhaps turning the conversation to the plight of a friend would keep Richard from pursuing whether Darcy had found a lady.

Richard laughed. "Bingley always thinks he has

found a lady. He is far too amiable." He took another swing at a bush. "But go on and tell me about her. What is she like?"

"Beautiful. Well-mannered. Amiable. However, she seemed indifferent, and so it was suggested that he forget her."

Richard stopped walking. A thought of a disturbing nature began to form in his mind as he recalled a discussion they had had on the way to Rosings. "This is the match you helped him avoid?"

Darcy nodded.

"So it was not her connections to which you objected?"

"No. I did not wish to see him in a marriage of unequal affections."

"And this lady was one he met in Hertfordshire?"

Darcy nodded. "Had she demonstrated even a small amount of preference, I would not have suggested a separation." He sighed. "I thought he would forget her. He has not."

Richard could not help noting the way Darcy spoke as if it were not just his friend who was affected. "Is there a way to discover if this lady was indeed indifferent or if a renewal of addresses might be welcomed?"

Darcy turned toward the parsonage that was just within view. "We could ask her sister."

"Miss Bennet?" asked Richard in surprise. Oh, this was becoming a complicated tangle to be unravelled if the Miss Bennet at the parsonage was the lady Darcy was considering marrying and if this Miss Bennet's sister had been injured by Bingley's removal from Netherfield. He shook his head as he realized that there might be one lady in all of England and its empire who would refuse a man like Darcy.

Chapter 2

Elizabeth Bennet rose as Colonel Fitzwilliam and Mr. Darcy entered the sitting room at the parsonage. She had known they were arriving and had expected them to call as was proper, but she had thought she would feel indifferent when it happened. However, that was not to be. Her heart had skittered and thumped when her cousin had announced that the gentlemen were approaching the parsonage. And now, upon their arrival, Elizabeth's eyes took in the smiling, though not entirely handsome countenance of Colonel Fitzwilliam, but it was a polite formality. Who she really wished to see was his cousin, Mr. Darcy. Her breath caught upon seeing him, and for once, Elizabeth was thankful for the constant chatter of her cousin, Mr. Collins, for it afforded her a moment to collect herself.

Mr. Darcy was as handsome and compelling as he had always been. He remained now, as he was the latest time they had met, an enigma. She had still not deciphered his character, and it was something which drew her curiosity. She had heard it both criticized and commended, but she had yet to decide which tale held the most weight. Certain aspects of Mr. Darcy's demeanor, as well as the slighting comment he had uttered at their first meeting, swayed her toward believing the worst of the man, but one of the sources of approbation, her sister Jane, caused Elizabeth to pause briefly in her judgment. Though she was nearly certain that Mr. Darcy was simply an arrogant man with little interest or feelings for those beneath him in status, she could not discount her sister's words.

"Miss Elizabeth," Darcy bowed as he greeted her. "I trust your family is well." He followed his cousin's suit and took a seat near her.

"The ones I left at Longbourn were in good spirits and health when I departed." She smiled as she said it, studying his face to see if it gave any indication of his knowing that not all her sisters were at Longbourn, but it did not. His brows furrowed in concern, and he seemed genuinely perplexed.

"Is not all your family at Longbourn?" He rubbed his hands on his thighs and willed himself to relax. She was as beautiful as he remembered, and her smile was enchanting.

Elizabeth shook her head. "Jane has been in London with my aunt and uncle for nearly three months now."

Darcy's brows rose, and his eyes widened. "In London for three months?"

There was no doubting that the gentleman in front of her did not know of Jane's stay in town. "You did not hear she had called on Mr. Bingley's sisters?

Darcy's heart dropped to his stomach. He had hoped to discern Jane's feelings for his friend, but he had not expected to be given such a ready example of her regard straightaway. He shook his head. "Miss Bingley made no mention of it to either myself or Mr. Bingley." He fidgeted with his sleeve. "Is your sister well?"

"She is not ill," Elizabeth replied with a tight smile. Jane's heart was broken, but her body was well.

Darcy tipped his head and looked very seriously at Elizabeth. "And her spirits?" The question was barely more than a whisper.

Richard saw the small quiver of Elizabeth's lip and the dampness in her eyes. The separation of Bingley from her sister had caused pain — a great deal of it, if he were reading things correctly.

"Improving," said Elizabeth.

"I wish I would have known she was in town," Darcy murmured.

Richard nearly groaned aloud at the look of incredulity Darcy's comment elicited from Elizabeth. This battle would not be easily won.

"You would have called on her? In Gracechurch Street? My relations are not among your equals." There was a sharpness to her tone.

Mr. Collins rattled the cup of tea he was about to hand to Mr. Darcy.

"You mean to say they are in trade?" Richard inserted as he saw Darcy recoil as if he had been slapped.

Elizabeth swallowed and her cheeks coloured slightly. She had forgotten she had an audience. "My uncle is in trade," she said, smoothing her skirt.

"Much like Bingley's father was?" Richard continued. He doubted that Elizabeth had thought her statement through, and he suspected he was correct when he saw her eyes widen just slightly.

"Yes, just so, but not so wealthy. I do not mean to say they are poor, but Mr. Bingley's fortune is substantial and therefore sets him apart,"' she explained.

"The nouveau riche," said Richard with a shrug. "The world is changing. Napoleon and those before him have seen to that." He raised a brow and scowled slightly. "Not to mention the Americans."

"We must change with the times," said Darcy. "And, yes, I would have called," he added. "Since I am not in town and cannot do my duty in calling on a friend, perhaps I could send Mr. Bingley in my stead? Would you allow me to inform him?"

Elizabeth could not believe what she was hearing. Mr. Darcy wanted to inform Mr. Bingley of Jane's presence in town? Was Mr. Darcy innocent of the charge she had laid at his feet of separating Jane from Mr. Bingley?

"Seeing a friend might lift your sister's spirits,

might it not?" asked Richard when no reply seemed forthcoming from Elizabeth.

"Oh, indeed, a call from a friend is always just the thing to lift anyone's spirits," said Mr. Collins. "And to have a call from someone such as the friend of one such as Mr. Darcy in such a place in town is not something at which to scoff. I am certain my cousin Jane knows her place and would feel the importance of such a call."

Richard saw Darcy's face darken. Mr. Collins was obviously a fool, and Richard knew how little tolerance Darcy had for fools. So, Richard smiled and replied before Darcy could. "I am relieved to know that Miss Bennet is a woman of sense. There are far too many nonsensical people in this world."

"There most certainly are," agreed Mr. Collins. And so began a lengthy commentary on what was and was not deemed foolish according to Mr. Collins, for the others could scarcely insert a word with the multitude that fell from the parson's lips.

Richard could tell by the twitch of Miss Elizabeth's lips and the twinkle in her eye that the absurdity of her cousin's speech was not lost on her. Finding it trying to listen to Mr. Collins, Richard began to make a mental assessment of the situation. Miss Elizabeth Bennet had been drawn to look at Darcy almost immediately upon his arrival. There was interest there. However, she seemed to have a poor opinion of Darcy's character. Such a thing was not entirely unexpected. Darcy's reserve often led people to believe he was proud. That would need some attention. Then there was the issue of the injured sister. He would allow Darcy to attempt to smooth that over. Miss Elizabeth had seemed startled into silence at the mention of a repair being made, so the breach may not be insurmountable.

At a rare pause in Mr. Collins's commentary, Richard followed Mrs. Collins's lead and chuckled at whatever it was that her husband had said. Miss Elizabeth's face shone with amusement. The lady possessed a sharp tongue and a keen wit. Darcy would not tire of such a woman as he did of the ladies of the ton, who had a limited ability to enter into debate. Richard suspected that Miss Elizabeth would not shy away from a debate. This was good.

He took a sip of his tea, satisfied with all the qualities he had observed in Miss Elizabeth. She was, as his aunt had declared, just the sort of lady Darcy should marry. And added to all these recommendations was the fact that she was compellingly pretty, and she affected his cousin in a way he had not heretofore seen. Darcy was uncomfortable around most ladies, but he did not dry his hands on his trousers or tug at his sleeves and cravat as he did in Miss Elizabeth's presence. The battle might not be easily won, but it would be a victory worth the effort.

Richard turned his attention back to the conversation at hand just as Mrs. Collins was interrupting her husband before he could venture off onto another topic which none but he cared to discuss.

"I trust your journey was good?" Charlotte asked, looking first at Darcy and then Richard.

"Oh, yes, how foolish of me not to remember to inquire," said Mr. Collins. "It is one of the many benefits of having a sensible bride." He took Charlotte's hand. "I tend to ramble, you know, but Mrs. Collins always knows how to bring me back to the point. I would highly recommend finding such a wife."

"Thank you, my dear," Charlotte replied, a hint of colour adding a bit of charm to her features.

How a sensible woman, such as Mrs. Collins

appeared to be, had ended up with such a husband as Mr. Collins and was able to seemingly enjoy his praise was beyond Richard's comprehension. But it could not be denied that there had been at least a few small looks and smiles shared between the two. They seemed genuinely content, if not happy.

"Our journey was without event," said Darcy.

"It was quite pleasant, even if I had to endure it with one so silent as my cousin," said Richard. It would do Miss Elizabeth good to see Darcy being teased.

"I was not silent," protested Darcy.

"No, not silent, but not talkative either." It was a prod to get Darcy to engage in a bit of banter.

Darcy's eyes narrowed, and he shook his head. "There was not silence enough for me to enter more than a few words."

Richard shrugged, pleased with the startled look the comment had drawn from Elizabeth. Yes, she needed to discover the less formal side of his cousin's character. "I do have a tendency to expound on many things."

Darcy chuckled. "No truer words have ever been spoken."

Elizabeth tilted her head and studied the man

seated to her left. She had never heard him chuckle or even appear to be slightly amused, and such a spectacle must be observed carefully, for she was not certain when it might happen again.

"And what sort of topics interest you, Colonel Fitzwilliam?" Elizabeth asked.

"Himself," muttered Darcy, his lips curling up in a hint of a smirk.

"I am of great interest," Richard agreed with aplomb. "My father supplies a good deal of material as do my brother and his children — he has two, an heir and an almost spare."

"An almost spare?" asked Maria, Mrs. Collins's younger sister, who was also staying at the parsonage.

Richard nodded. "She is a second child, but she is not a son and cannot inherit the title, so Millicent is the almost spare."

"That is horrid," said Maria with all the indignation a lady of sixteen could muster.

"I do not make the rules for inheritance," replied Richard. "My brother and his wife were so certain that their second child was to be a boy that when Millie was born and not a boy, the moniker just seemed appropriate." He winked. "She is only two, so the name does not bother her in the least. Her father is not so complacent, and it is for his sake that I use it."

"I still think it horrid," protested Maria.

"As does my sister," said Darcy. "Georgiana is forever scolding Richard for saying it, but in my cousin's defence, he never uses it in Millicent's presence. It is truly only a phrase to torment the viscount."

"Then, I should like Miss Darcy quite well for rendering such a service on behalf of her little cousin." Maria's chin lifted as she said it, and Mr. Collins cleared his throat uneasily.

"I think you would like Georgiana regardless of her scolding of me," said Richard. "She is a shy girl, but sincere and loyal — traits that run true in our family. One such as yourself could not go wrong in befriending her."

"Miss Darcy has a tender heart, it would seem," said Charlotte.

"Yes," replied Darcy. "Georgiana possesses a very affectionate heart."

Elizabeth's brows furrowed slightly. This description did not match that of Mr. Wickham's. Wickham had claimed Miss Darcy was proud and cold. But then, she was currently being described by her relations and there must be some allowance for prejudice. It was only natural and proper.

Richard checked his watch. Miss Elizabeth was looking confused enough that it might be best to take their leave while she was still feeling unsettled. "It has been a pleasure," he said as he snapped the cover closed over his watch, "and I am given to understand that you will be joining us for dinner."

"Oh, indeed," said Mr. Collins. "Lady Catherine is very gracious in her attentions."

"I am certain she is," Richard said as he stood to take his leave. He had no desire to hear the man launch into an exaltation of Lady Catherine's finer qualities.

"If you would be so kind as to give me your uncle's address for Mr. Bingley's knowledge," said Darcy as he followed his cousin's lead and stood.

Elizabeth blinked. He truly did mean to send Mr. Bingley to call on Jane. "Of course, if you will give me a moment, I shall write it out for you."

"We shall await you outside," said Richard, moving to the door and giving Darcy no choice but to follow, which he did.

They had been in the front garden no more than five minutes listening to Mr. Collins elaborate on the flowers, when Elizabeth, thankfully, appeared, and they were free to return to Rosings — Darcy to write his letter to Bingley and the colonel to consult with his aunt.

Chapter 3

Elizabeth could not for any inducement come to a conclusion on what manner of man Mr. Darcy was. When he had called at the parsonage yesterday, he had been amiable and polite. He had even inquired after her sister and offered to reunite Jane with Mr. Bingley. Yet, he had stood so aloof in Hertfordshire — silent and grave, often casting a disparaging eye on his surroundings. There were also Mr. Wickham's claims of Darcy's ill-treatment to consider.

How she wished that Jane were here to discuss the matter. Charlotte was a dear friend, but she was not Jane. Therefore, there was little that could be done aside from pondering and observing, which would have been easier to do last evening if Colonel Fitzwilliam had allowed it. The colonel was a pleasant gentleman, and having an amiable gentleman, who also happened to be the second son of an earl, flirting with you was not disagreeable unless you desired peace to order your thinking.

It was also not helpful that the agreeable and engaging Mr. Darcy from the afternoon's call had been replaced by the scowling and sullen gentleman she had often encountered in Hertfordshire.

Elizabeth paced a circle around a bench at the far edge of Rosings' garden. Thanks to Colonel Fitzwilliam and Mr. Collins, Lady Catherine had learned last evening that Elizabeth enjoyed walking and had insisted that her morning constitutional include a tour of Rosings' gardens. Elizabeth had tried to refuse, but it was not to be. Mr. Collins would not hear of it, and having both Lady Catherine and Mr. Collins put out with her was not something Elizabeth wished to endure. She made one last turn around the bench before taking a seat.

She had to admit that the view from here was spectacular. From this particular spot, she could see down a soft incline to a pond and a folly beyond. A bird hopped out from under a bush, catching her attention for a moment before she looked back toward the folly. Tomorrow, she would have to venture to it.

"Miss Bennet."

Elizabeth jumped at the sound of her name.

"I do apologize for startling you. It was not my intent." Anne de Bourgh took a seat next to Elizabeth. "This is my favourite prospect."

"It is lovely." Elizabeth could easily see why this would be a favourite view.

"I have tried to capture it many times, but I fear my skills are not what they should be." She lay the notebook she was hugging to her chest on the bench. "Mother had someone in to teach me, but I would have excelled more had I been exposed to the masters in town." She shifted so that she was turned slightly toward Elizabeth and away from the folly. "However, my health is best in the country. The foul air of town is draining. It is so hard to breathe there."

"The air is rather stale at times," Elizabeth agreed.

Anne laughed. "You are too polite. The air is vile, which is why I will never live there." She smiled at Elizabeth. "In fact, I intend never to leave

Kent. I would dislike being any distance from my mother. She and Mr. James, the apothecary, know best how to help me when I become ill. I would trust none other."

Elizabeth's brows furrowed. Where not Miss de Bourgh and Mr. Darcy betrothed? How would Miss de Bourgh be able to stay in Kent once she married Mr. Darcy? Elizabeth placed a hand on her heart as it pinched with sadness. It was strange that it should hurt just now. She attempted to focus her attention on the view before her, but her curiosity would not be quelled without knowing the answer to her questions.

"Forgive me if I am impertinent, but are you not betrothed to Mr. Darcy?" Elizabeth asked, the strange, sad pinching repeated itself.

"You have heard of that?" Anne asked in surprise.

"I have," Elizabeth admitted.

Anne sighed and smiled. "From Mr. Collins most likely."

"Yes, he was one source." Elizabeth bit her lip. She should have just acknowledged the truth of Miss de Bourgh's statement with a simple yes. There was no need to bring up the fact that she had listened to Mr. Wickham's tales, and yet, that seemed to be exactly what she was doing.

"And the other?" Anne's eyes were wide with interest.

"Someone who claims a long acquaintance with Mr. Darcy." It was not enough of an answer. Miss de Bourgh waited expectantly for a name. Elizabeth looked down at her hands, embarrassment stealing its way across her cheeks. "Mr. Wickham."

"That scoundrel!" declared Miss de Bourgh. "It is best not to believe more than half the words that come from his mouth."

Elizabeth could not contain her shock. "He seemed charming."

Anne laughed bitterly. "Oh, he is charming. He will charm a lady right out of her stays and stockings and leave her smiling until she realizes he will not be returning — unless she has a fortune. Then, he will return, but it will not be for her. It will be for the gold in her possession."

Elizabeth gasped.

"I assure you it is true. I cannot give particulars, but rest assured, he is no friend of Darcy's — not any longer, at least."

Elizabeth did not know what to say. She had been so certain that Wickham was trustworthy. He had smiled and whispered in such a believable way.

"Why Darcy did not run that blackguard through for his treachery, I do not know," continued Anne. "If I were a man and had been so ill-used, I would have."

Elizabeth shook her head. Miss de Bourgh's words did not match with what Elizabeth had heard from Mr. Wickham. "Mr. Darcy was ill-used, not Mr. Wickham?" She wrapped an arm around her stomach, which was turning most unpleasantly, and tears gathered along the rims of her eyes. If what Miss de Bourgh was telling her was true, she had been most assuredly fooled. Mr. Wickham had spoken so firmly, so clearly, so lacking in anything but assurance that his story was correct.

Anne's expression softened as she took in Elizabeth's state of shock. "Mr. Wickham is a master storyteller, is he not?"

Elizabeth nodded and blinked, but instead of dispersing her tears, the action caused one to roll down her cheek.

"I would tell you the true tale, but Darcy might

not approve. It is his story to tell, after all, and of a delicate nature."

Elizabeth wiped at the offending tear. Her mind returned to her original question. "So you are not betrothed to Mr. Darcy?"

Anne smiled and picked up her notebook. "He has never asked, and I have never accepted."

"Would you?" the question escaped Elizabeth before she could think better of it. Why she felt compelled to know this bit of information, she did not know. Curiosity, she supposed. She had always been a curious creature.

Anne shook her head. "No. He has homes in London and in Derbyshire. Neither is close to Rosings." She took a pencil out of her reticule. "And I do not love him. I would prefer a love match."

Elizabeth did not know what to think. The world seemed to be standing on its head. Mr. Wickham was a scoundrel who had used Darcy poorly. Miss de Bourgh was not betrothed to Mr. Darcy. Mr. Darcy seemed genuinely concerned with Jane's well-being. None of these things supported any of her previous suppositions. "It is most startling," she muttered as Miss de Bourgh looked at her surreptitiously.

"I suppose it is." Anne turned her focus back to the view in front of her and applied herself to her drawing.

Elizabeth sighed, her shoulders drooping under the weight of these new revelations and what they said about her ability to judge character. Most often, her evaluation of a person was accurate. Had she not deemed Mr. Walters a cad and a gambler, and had he not proven to be such? Had she not declared Miss Palmer to be the only lady worthy of the parish rector's affections, and had she not turned out to be precisely the best woman to fill the position of parson's wife? Was Miss Palmer not now the most compassionate person to all those who called at the parsonage with a need? So why was Elizabeth now stumbling so seriously in her abilities to decipher character?

It was humiliating, really, to be so very wrong. Elizabeth refused to ponder it further, for if she were to start by admitting that she had been incorrect about Mr. Darcy and Mr. Wickham, she would then have to evaluate her actions towards each gentleman. And if being wrong in one's estimation of another's character was humiliating, viewing your poor behaviour based on that estimation was thoroughly shameful.

Elizabeth remained silently on the bench next to Miss de Bourgh for a full five more uneasy minutes before excusing herself and beginning her walk back to the parsonage. As she rounded a turn in the grove, she came to a full stop. Miss de Bourgh had not said everything Mr. Wickham said was to be discounted. Surely, there must be some small portion of truth in what Mr. Wickham said that made his story plausible.

As she continued walking, she reviewed all that Mr. Wickham had told her. Mr. Wickham had claimed Mr. Darcy to be both proud in his actions toward others and cruel in withholding a living. Now she wondered if perhaps the living had been withheld because of whatever had happened between them. Not that such a fact did Mr. Darcy any credit. A vengeful spirit was not complimentary to a gentleman, but it was possible that Mr. Darcy had given the living to another as a reprisal for whatever wrong Mr. Wickham had committed.

Next, she considered the greeting she had

observed between the two gentlemen when they had met in Hertfordshire. It had been unpleasant at best. In fact, it had seemed rather filled with loathing. And she, herself, knew from that first assembly that Mr. Darcy could be very haughty and even rude. These facts were also not credits to Mr. Darcy's character.

She paused before exiting the grove and returning to the parsonage. It must be the general disagreeableness of Mr. Darcy's personality and his unwillingness to restore a person to favour once his good opinion had been lost on which the whole of Mr. Wickham's story was built. If it were not true that Mr. Darcy was arrogant and had Mr. Darcy's actions in Hertfordshire been more unpretentious, not a word of Mr. Wickham's story would be believable.

She smiled, relieved that she had finally deciphered something about the man from Derbyshire and that she had not been entirely wrong in her assessment of him. He was proud and arrogant. That remained true.

She bit her lip as a pang of something stabbed at her heart. It did remain true, did it not? She shook her head. It would not do to be so wavering. She would leave room to shift her opinion if it became obvious that it was not correct, but for now, she would hold to her assessment — Mr. Darcy was proud and arrogant. This was, after all, based not only on the words of Mr. Wickham but also on Mr. Darcy's actions. Had he not slighted her most grievously? Had he not worn a disdainful look frequently? Yes, she told herself, rubbing softly at her heart, it must be true.

Chapter 4

Darcy turned his horse toward the stables. He had thought to walk in the grove this morning with the hope of finding Elizabeth there, but having seen her smile and laugh at his cousin last night, coupled with the comments Richard had made this morning regarding Elizabeth, Darcy had decided a long, hard ride would be better.

Of course, Darcy knew Elizabeth's eyes were expressive and captivating. He did not need his cousin to point that out. Nor did he need Richard to alert him to the fact that Elizabeth was witty and charming. Darcy knew these things. She was blasted enchanting for heaven's sake! That is why he was considering asking her to marry him. She had captivated his heart and mind, and he could not remove her from either — no matter how hard he had tried to do just that.

He slowed his horse. He had no desire yet to see Richard. A brief time in the garden or near the folly might ease his mind a bit more. It would do no good to be agitated in his aunt's presence, for she would badger him until he said something unflattering or told her the very thing that was bothering him. He sighed.

Lady Catherine was not horrid — she just was not always pleasant. He chuckled to himself. He was not certain many would agree with him. The woman was demanding and imperious, but she had also taken both him and his sister in for a few months after their mother's death to give their father time to grieve in private. She had been mostly understanding.

He swung down off his horse and took a seat on the second step to the folly. Lady Catherine had not once said negative things about boys not crying or keeping a stiff upper lip. She had allowed Darcy to express his grief and had even held him in a firm, if somewhat rigid, embrace while he had wept for his mother. No, she was not horrid.

It was also here that had been a safe haven for Georgiana after her ordeal at Ramsgate. Lady Catherine had limited herself to only one small lecture on propriety before seeing Georgiana set on a path to recover her spirits. In fact, Mrs. Annesley, one of Mrs. Jenkinson's nieces, had been employed as Georgiana's companion on Lady Catherine's recommendation. He shook his head. At times, his aunt could be very helpful and caring. It was unfortunate that she chose to hide such qualities most times in favour of meddling in the affairs of others and arranging them in what she considered a better fashion.

Darcy squinted, peering toward the bottom of the garden. Anne was there per her normal habit, but she was not alone. He smiled. Perhaps, he would be fortunate enough to see Elizabeth after all.

He rose and began leading his horse toward the garden. He would find a gardener to see his mount returned to the stables. If Darcy were quick enough, he might be allowed the privilege of walking Elizabeth back to the parsonage. Such a walk would afford him the chance to see if his addresses might be welcomed.

Fortunately, he was able to locate a gardener, who was willing to put aside his work for a few moments to return a horse to the stables. Darcy slowly approached the bench where his cousin sat. It was not fear or nerves that caused him to be unhurried. No, he was enjoying the view of Elizabeth with her bonnet in her lap and her cheeks glowing from activity. It was captivating. He stopped a short distance away so that he might just admire her for a moment.

There was something wrong. Her head was lowered, and she occasionally brushed at her eye as if drying a tear. He began walking toward her again, but she stood and with a hasty curtsey, began walking away toward the grove. She had looked his direction and fled. His heart sank, and turning, he returned to the house to seek solace in the library.

He was just finishing a third chapter in his book when Richard gave a loud rap at the door and allowed himself entry before Darcy could either grant or refuse it.

"Aunt Catherine requires our presence for tea." He plopped into a chair next to Darcy. "The ladies from the parsonage are expected."

Darcy glanced up from his book and gave a quick smile of acknowledgement. "I will attend her when I have finished what I was about."

Richard's brows rose. Darcy was supposed to be eager to see Miss Elizabeth. He was certain that Darcy had flown off on a ride in a fit of jealousy this morning.

"I am certain you can entertain the ladies until I arrive." Darcy lifted a not entirely amused brow. "You did a capable job of it last night."

Richard smiled. Ah, his cousin was jealous. "It was not so hard. They seemed eager for some lively discussion, and there were no other gentlemen willing to provide it."

Darcy rolled his eyes. "You know I am not so comfortable in social settings as you are."

Richard shrugged. "You seemed at ease when we visited the parsonage. I had almost imagined you were interested in Miss Elizabeth." He studied Darcy's face for the telltale flinch of his jaw muscle that always told Richard when he had hit upon the truth of a matter that Darcy was trying to conceal. There. Just then. Was that not a flinch? Richard was almost certain it was.

Darcy returned his eyes to his book. "I had almost expected a proposal from you last night. Your advances were not subtle."

Richard bit back a smile. Darcy was more than

jealous. He was provoked. The thought should not have pleased Richard so much as it did. However, Darcy was not easily riled, so it was a sort of accomplishment. "She is lovely," he said thoughtfully, steepling his fingers and resting his chin on them as if considering the lady.

"She is not for you," said Darcy.

"And why not?" asked Richard, purposefully knocking his foot against Darcy's leg as he extended his feet and crossed them.

"Your father would not approve." Darcy snapped his book closed and glowered at Richard. Why must his cousin carry on as if he was actually considering Elizabeth as a potential bride. Had Richard not always claimed a lady's first and most important qualifying asset be her dowry? Surely, he knew Miss Elizabeth was not an heiress. "Nor would you."

Richard chuckled. "And, pray tell, what makes Miss Elizabeth unacceptable?"

Upon hearing her name, Elizabeth froze outside the half-open door to the library. Charlotte gave her a quizzical look. Elizabeth held a finger to her lips.

"Her portion is not ideal." Darcy refused to

comment on the size of it in particular, for to him and many a gentleman with a good inheritance, it was not beyond consideration. However, to Richard, who claimed to wish for an heiress to allow him to live in a style to which he was accustomed, it was not enough.

"A small matter," said Richard, struggling to keep from smiling at the narrowing of Darcy's brows. Clearly, his cousin was smitten.

"Her family has ties to trade." He lifted an eyebrow at Richard. Lord Matlock was not backwards in his thinking, but some of his trusted political allies were.

"That should not be an issue unless running for parliament, and even then it is not insurmountable," Richard retorted with a shrug.

Darcy lowered his voice. The only other reason he could think of to use to dissuade his cousin was not a flattering one, and he did not wish to have anyone overhear him say it. However, his voice was not quite low enough for Elizabeth's keen sense of hearing.

"Her family — her mother, in particular, tends toward the ridiculous in a loud and tactless fashion. Her younger sisters are ill-behaved, and her father does naught to stop them. I believe he finds humor in their antics." Darcy's heart raced as he spoke the words. Though true, they were cruel.

Elizabeth closed her eyes against the pain of his words. She was right. He was proud, arrogant, and heartless.

"Come," whispered Charlotte. "Lady Catherine will be wondering what has caused our delay."

Elizabeth nodded and followed her friend.

"You do not know the context of the conversation, " Charlotte cautioned as they entered the sitting room. "Withhold judgment until you do."

"There is no context in which such a conversation is acceptable," muttered Elizabeth.

"Ah, finally, you have arrived," Lady Catherine motioned for them to join her. "Miss Maria thought you had run off and left her on her own." Her tone was slightly teasing, a fact that would have startled Elizabeth as much as her companions if she had been listening. However, Elizabeth's mind was still in the hall outside the library door.

"Elizabeth had a pebble in her shoe," said Charlotte, tugging Elizabeth by the arm and leading her to a chair. "She is a bit out of sorts. I think her walk was a bit too long this morning." Charlotte gave Elizabeth a pleading look.

Elizabeth smiled. "Indeed, I am a trifle fatigued today. It is most unusual."

"Did you sleep well?" Lady Catherine questioned. "It is not unusual to sleep ill when not in your own bed although I do believe the beds at the parsonage are as comfortable as any in a proper house."

"Oh, they are, my lady, " Maria assured Lady Catherine. "I have slept very well. Better than when I am at home, in fact."

"They are most comfortable," Elizabeth assured Lady Catherine. "I do not recall sleeping poorly, but it might have happened that my sleep was lighter than it is usually wont to be."

Lady Catherine tilted her head. "Tomorrow, you should not walk. You should apply yourself to something of beauty that is not a walk." Her eyes narrowed a moment. "The piano. You said you lack technique due to negligence in practice."

"Oh, I am certain I will be well tomorrow," Elizabeth protested.

"Even if you are," Lady Catherine said with a stern look, "I will expect you at half eleven to practice. There is a piano in an empty room upstairs that you may use without being disturbed or in anyone's way."

Elizabeth knew that to protest was of little use. Lady Catherine looked determined, and even Elizabeth's courage was not strong enough to protest such a look over something as simple as practising. "Thank you, my lady."

"Anne," Lady Catherine continued, "you will inform Mrs. Jenkinson that Georgiana's music is to be left on the piano." She turned to Elizabeth. "Mrs. Jenkinson has a piano in her room, you see, and she has been using the music. Anne attempted to learn the instrument, but alas, it was not in the talents the Lord gave her. You, on the other hand, show potential. There is expression in your playing that cannot be denied. If you were not so overcome today, I would have greatly liked to hear you play."

Elizabeth accepted the compliment and then turned her full attention to her tea and a discussion that Maria was having with Miss de Bourgh when the gentlemen entered the room. She dared not look at him, for she was certain that either her face would display her loathing or her tumultuous emotions would spill down her cheeks.

Darcy watched her. There was indeed something amiss. In all the time he had spent in Elizabeth's presence, he never once remembered her adding so little to a conversation. And she would not lift her eyes to him except for the briefest of moments. Richard, however, seemed worthy of a smile and a tease. It was enough to send Darcy from the room before it was entirely proper.

He paced his room when he reached it. Richard could complete the yearly reviews and tours without him. Darcy would stay one more day, but then he would find a reason to escape. He could not remain where he was forced to watch her attachment to another grow. He sank down on the edge of his bed. One more day. Surely, he could endure one more day.

Chapter 5

Lady Catherine motioned for Richard to take a seat next to her at the table. "You have his key?"

Richard shook his head. "Not yet, but I will as soon as he has returned and his man has made his bath ready."

Lady Catherine raised a brow at him as she took a sip of her tea.

"I will have it," Richard assured her. He knew a thing or two about Darcy, and one of those things was that the key to Darcy's room never left his sight unless he was taking a bath. It was likely due to the fact that ladies such as Miss Bingley were actively trying to ensnare his fortune. To have taken the key this morning or even last evening when he had been in Darcy's room would have alerted his cousin that something was afoot. And that would not do.

"Was he still in high dudgeon this morning?" Lady Catherine placed her empty cup on the table.

Richard nodded. "I could barely draw more than a dozen words from him, and the majority of those words were not at all nice or proper."

"Did you have to flirt with her so much?" Lady Catherine gave him a mildly disapproving look. It was not the first time she had questioned her decision to involve Richard in her plan. He was so much like his father.

How many times had she and her sister endured their brother's merciless teasing until one or the other quit the room in a huff or succumbed to tears. It was as if he could not or would not read the signs that he had pushed too far. He was always repentant, however, and after he had married, he had finally learned the acceptable bounds between being mildly annoying and utterly provoking. She credited Lady Matlock with that accomplishment. Richard did seem able to reign his pestering on most occasions and especially with the fairer sex, but when it came to his brother or Darcy, he occasionally overstepped his bounds. From the way Darcy had left the room yesterday and been silent and disagreeable the rest of the day,

Lady Catherine was certain Richard had indeed pushed Darcy well past any tolerable limit.

"It was what you said to do!" And it had been a pleasant enough task. Miss Elizabeth was delightful and being a burr under Darcy's saddle was always good for a smile or two. However, he did have to admit, he had never seen Darcy quite as put out as he currently was — at least not by something Richard had done. Wickham — well, there was a man who could cause as much consternation as Darcy presently displayed. Perhaps, Richard had gone a bit too far in his game. The purpose of the attack was, after all, to provoke not decimate.

Lady Catherine sighed. "True. At least, we know I was correct in my assessment of his attachment to the young lady. He is half in love with her already."

Richard laughed. "No, my dear aunt, you are incorrect. He is completely besotted. He even tried to tell me why I should not pursue her and in a very high and mighty fashion — condemning her connections and her family. The whole while he was rubbing his hands on his pants and tugging at his collar." He leaned back in his chair. "Darcy has never been good at speaking ill of one he cares about."

"That is because he is a proper gentleman." Lady Catherine's chin rose as she said it. "My sister would not have raised him to be anything less." Her eyes narrowed slightly as her lips curled in a teasing smile. "Unlike my brother."

Richard's mouth dropped open. "I am capable of being a proper gentleman. I just choose not to be. It is so dull."

Lady Catherine chuckled. "That is precisely what my brother would tell our father."

Richard shrugged. There was no denying his father and he were alike both in looks and temperament. And as far as he was concerned, that was not an imperfection. Quite the contrary! His father was well-liked and successful and not solely because he was an earl but because he was an earl with an exceptional character and a pleasant personality.

Lady Catherine looked at the clock. "Miss Bennet will be here in one hour to practice."

Richard gave a sharp nod of his head. "Darcy will be back in half an hour if he is holding to schedule, which I assume he is."

Lady Catherine rose from her seat. "Collins will be bringing me his sermon at two, and we will take tea together. Do not be late."

Richard smiled. This was a tea he would not miss for any inducement, for it promised to be a memorable affair.

~*~*~

Elizabeth stopped at the gates to Rosings. She did not want to practice, and she most decidedly did not want to enter that house. She did not even wish to be on the grounds. It was all in too close a proximity to that man. She stood for three minutes complete, contemplating if refusing to do as Lady Catherine had directed was worth the long and nonsensical scolding she would receive from her cousin. Being barred from Rosings was not a threat but rather a consequence for which to wish. How was she to even look at Mr. Darcy with any sort of composure after hearing what she had heard? And to think she had been considering that he might not be as horrid as she had first deemed!

She shook her head. Feigning civility even to the likes of Mr. Darcy was better than enduring a diatribe from her cousin, for she knew that it would not be one rebuke but an unending litany recited and expanded upon as each new day dawned. So, with an enormous sigh, she lifted her chin and march to her doom.

"Good morning, Miss Elizabeth," Richard greeted her as she came near the house.

Elizabeth curtseyed and returned the greeting. "I am here to practice as I was instructed to do."

There was something not entirely pleasant about Miss Elizabeth this morning. Her eyes were dull, and her smile had no spark. "My aunt can be demanding." He tilted his head and studied her expression. "You are not unwell, are you?"

"A slight headache," Elizabeth admitted. "However, it is not enough to render me unable to please my cousin's patroness." She had attempted to use her headache as a reason to avoid Rosings, but Mr. Collins would not hear of it. According to him, a bit of music would likely cure all her ills if the glorious walk to Rosings, knowing the favour of one so great as Lady Catherine had been bestowed upon her, did not do so first. She smiled sheepishly. "My cousin can also be demanding."

Richard chuckled and accepted the explanation but felt that more was amiss. However, there was no way to inquire further without being thought meddlesome. He extended an arm to her. "Allow me to escort you to your instrument."

Elizabeth could not help smiling at the flourish of his free hand as he waved it toward the house. Why could his cousin not be so amiable? It was as if the two were opposites sides of the same coin — one dour and grave and the other affable and bright.

"I must admit that I am selfish enough to be grateful for my aunt's insistence that you play. There are far too many stays here that are dull. A new friend and music do lend a certain delight to this visit." He led her up the grand staircase and toward the family wing. "It is only when Mrs. Jenkinson is required to play, or Georgiana is with us, that there is anything as pleasant as music about the house."

"No one else plays?"

Richard shook his head. "Anne's skill at the piano was passed on to her by her mother," he leaned closer and whispered, "No matter how much Aunt Catherine insists she would have been a proficient had she practiced, it was not meant to be — or so my father says. But, you mustn't tell her I said so, for I will deny it if you do."

He turned as his batman, Mr. Stone, approached. "Did you find the missing item?" he inquired but then, held up a hand to prevent the man from answering. He needed Elizabeth only to hear a reason for his leaving her to find the piano on her own. He did not need her to hear any of the discussion about the item that was missing because it had been taken at his request.

He turned to Elizabeth. "I must apologize. There is a matter that requires my attention. Three doors up on the left is where you will find what you need."

"Oh, of course," Elizabeth replied.

Richard turned toward Mr. Stone but not so far as to not be able to see Miss Elizabeth's progress. "You have the keys?"

Mr. Stone handed two keys to Richard.

"And the bell?"

"Disconnected," said Mr. Stone.

"From all three rooms," Richard began moving down the hall as Elizabeth reached the door he had directed her toward.

"Yes, sir."

"And Darcy's man?"

"Resting uneasily below stairs but unwilling to cross Lady Catherine."

"He knows the purpose, does he not?" Richard stopped and waited until Elizabeth had entered the room he had told her contained the piano and then hurried toward the door and carefully locked it almost as soon as it closed.

"He does," whispered Mr. Stone, "but he fears he will lose his spot. I assured him that you and Lady Catherine would not allow it, yet he is nervous."

Richard pulled his man down the hall toward the servant's stairs. "No one is to open that door or the two next to it."

"The instructions have been given," Mr. Stone assured him. "No one is to come to this floor until you have given the go ahead."

"Very good." Richard turned and looked back toward the door he had just locked. The handle was jiggling, and there was a soft knocking. Oh, Darcy and Miss Elizabeth would be angry. He blew out a breath. "I do hope they are in a forgiving mood once they are released."

Mr. Stone chuckled. "I would have thought you would have considered that before undertaking this scheme."

"You can be replaced," Richard growled.

Mr. Stone shook his head. "No, I cannot. Your father has promised my father that I will be your man for the duration of our stay in his majesty's forces." He grinned at Richard's sly smile. "However, I realize that you could make my stay unbearable, so I will wish you well in this endeavour. I await your command." He saluted smartly and, pivoting on his heel, left Richard to watch the hall on his own.

Richard pulled a sofa that stood near the servant's stairs directly in front of the door to the stairs and took a seat. It would be a long watch, but he must be certain that no one interfered with the plans that had been set in motion.

"They are captured?" Anne asked quietly, poking her head out of her room just down the hall.

He waved for her to join him. "They are. There has been rattling of the door and a few knocks, but nothing further."

"Darcy has not bellowed?"

Richard chuckled. "Not yet, and I am fairly certain it will be a while before he does since he is likely improperly dressed."

Anne's eyes sparkled. "Do tell."

Richard leaned back and patted the seat next to him.

Chapter 6

Elizabeth closed the door to the room. It was nicely furnished with a couch and chair in front of the fireplace and a lovely writing desk under the window. However, this was as much as she could see from the entry way since an armoire blocked her view of the rest of the room. The piano must be on the other side of that armoire.

She stepped around the piece of furniture and stopped. There was no piano. There was instead, a very large bed with a trunk at its foot and a set of clothes laid out on the mattress — a set of men's clothes. And boots. There were boots standing next to a chair beside the bed.

With her hand resting on her racing heart, Elizabeth turned back to the door. She had counted three doors up on the left. She was certain of it. She tried the handle on the door, but it would not turn. She pulled harder and then knocked softly as panic began to demand larger breaths to keep her head from spinning.

"Richard, is that you?"

Elizabeth's heart lurched. No, no, no. This could not be his room. It could not be!

"Richard?" Darcy called as he entered his room, rubbing his head with a towel.

Elizabeth dropped her gaze to the ground. Mr. Darcy was dressed only in a robe, and she was standing in his room. Oh, how she wished the floor would open up and drop her to her death. That would be far less painful than forcing a "No, it is not Richard" from her lips. However, the floor did not open, and her teeth, tongue, and lips managed to produce the sounds needed to alert him to her presence. She covered her face with her hands.

"The door is locked. I cannot leave," she added to her admission that she was not Richard.

"Miss Elizabeth?"

"I am afraid that is my name," she replied, turning away from him. "Colonel Fitzwilliam told me that this was the room where I could find the piano. Your aunt insists that I practice, and my cousin would not allow me to remain at home, even if my head did hurt."

Darcy tied the rope around his waist more snuggly.

"I was in the hall, and a man came up to Colonel Fitzwilliam, and there was something that was lost, and he told me to go three doors up on the left, so I did, and then I entered and rounded the wardrobe," she waved her hand behind her at the large piece of furniture as she babbled, "and there was no piano. I tried to leave, but the door will not open."

He pushed by her and tried the handle for himself. It was indeed locked. "You do not have the key?"

"Why should I have the key?" she retorted, looking at him with wide eyes. "It is not my room."

Darcy raised a brow. "You would not be the first lady to attempt to snare a gentleman in such a fashion." He clamped his lips closed and moved passed her again to go look for the key. He should not have said that. She was not the sort to affect a compromise — at least not with him. Besides, if she were to attempt to snare anyone in this house, it would be Richard. Darcy pulled out drawers and searched for the key. Not finding it anywhere in his dresser, he got down on his knees and felt under the bed.

"You think I would try to trap you?" Elizabeth had finally found her voice after such a startling accusation. "If it were my intent to do so, I would have done it while at Netherfield, but why should I want to be tied to you?" She folded her arms and glared at him. Her anger overcoming her embarrassment at seeing him dressed as he was with his bare feet and calves poking out from under his robe as knelt on the floor. "I should hope to marry a man with some sensibility, or at least, one who knows how to smile."

"Thank you for clarifying your opinion of me." He rose from the floor and rounding the bed to the far side of the room opened a door. "You will find a piano in here. There is a sitting room between my room and the room my sister uses when she is here." He stepped back and waited for Elizabeth to cross the room and go through the door. Then, he closed it and leaned against it. He was correct in one thing, she disliked him. He pushed off the door and gathered up his clothes, taking them to the dressing room to attempt to make himself somewhat presentable.

Elizabeth stood just inside the sitting room. Her anger fading and a strange sadness filling her heart. Mr. Darcy had not raised his voice in return to her harsh words. He had merely replied softly as if what she had said had cut him to the core. She would have preferred him to bluster about. She bit her lip and looked back at the door to his room and then crossed to the instrument.

A small pile of music lay neatly on the side, and one piece was spread out as if waiting for her to attempt it. Her eyes ran over the notes as they rose and fell on the staff. It was not a simple piece, but it was not completely beyond her skills. She began by picking out the notes on the upper staff with her right hand. Then, reaching the end of the piece, she did the same with her left hand before attempting to combine the two.

Darcy heard her slowly picking out the tune of a familiar song as he dressed. It reminded him of hearing Georgiana approach a new composition. How he loved to watch her tip her head and bite her lip as she concentrated on learning the fingering and committing the melody to memory.

He wondered if Elizabeth did the same. He pulled on one stocking and then another. His boots he would do without, just as he would do without his jacket and cravat. He pulled a pocket knife out of his dresser and attempted to force the lock open on his door, but it was of no use. He returned the knife to its drawer and sank into a chair by the fireplace. He would read until she left, then he would ring for his man and make himself presentable in time for tea.

For twenty minutes Darcy stared at a book and thought about the lady in the other room. For the same twenty minutes, Elizabeth attempted to apply herself to her music but found her mind wandering to the gentleman beyond the door. He was insufferable, she reminded herself. Handsome and wealthy, but insufferable. Finally, she rose from the instrument.

She had practised as required. Neither Lady Catherine nor Mr. Collins had indicated how long she had to play. She pulled on the door to the room, but it did not budge. She pulled harder but without success.

There was yet another door she could try — the one in Miss Darcy's bedroom. She hurried through the door that adjoined the sitting room and tried Miss Darcy's door. It, like all the others, would not budge. With a resigned sigh, she returned to the piano and sat on the bench but did not touch the keys. She was trapped — well and truly trapped. There was no way to leave these rooms without someone coming to let her out.

In the other room, Darcy snapped his book closed. He had not heard a door open or close, but she was not playing, so she must have left. He pulled his bell and then went to the sitting room door and peeked in. Elizabeth sat at the instrument, her hands covering her face, and her shoulders rising and falling as she cried. No matter what she had said to him. No matter what she thought of him, he could not allow her to go uncomforted.

"Miss Elizabeth," he said softly as he approached her, "are you well?" It was a silly thing to say when a lady was weeping, but what else could he ask?

She rubbed the tears from her cheeks with her hands and shrugged. "They are all locked."

He handed her a handkerchief and took the chair next to the piano where he always sat to turn pages for his sister. "What are all locked?"

"The doors." Her reply was somewhat muffled by the cloth she was using to dry her face.

"This door?" he asked.

She nodded. "And the one in Miss Darcy's room. We are trapped."

The oddness of the situation settled uneasily around Darcy. Three doors locked, and no keys to open them? He knew that the keys for this room and Georgiana's were kept by the housekeeper and Lady Catherine unless Georgiana was in residence. The fact that the door to this room had not been left unlocked if it was intended to be the room where Elizabeth practiced did not make sense.

"I have rung for my man," he said. "When he comes, you will be able to escape."

"From your room?" She blew her nose softly.

"Yes."

"And if someone sees me exiting your room? What then?"

He sighed. "That would be up to you." He would marry her, but only if she wished it. He would not force her. The situation might be able to be covered.

"Me?"

He nodded.

"There would be no option. We would have to marry." The thought did not terrify her as much as she had expected. Mr. Darcy was a sullen, arrogant man, but surely, he would be kind to his wife.

"Only if you wished it. I would not force my disagreeable self on you." There was a touch of bitterness in his tone.

"You would leave me a ruined woman?"

He shook his head. "No, I would never do anything to harm you. I would see that the story was not spread, and you would be free to choose whomever you wished."

She tipped her head and looked at him. "Truly?"

His smile was quick and sad. "Though it would break my heart, yes." He rose and paced to the window. "Richard has a small inheritance and a pension."

She stared after him. Did he mean that he wished to marry her? That was not possible. "My connections are unsuitable," she said, "and my family ridiculous." She wiped at her eyes again. His second comment finally took root in her thinking. "Colonel Fitzwilliam?"

He glanced over his shoulder towards her. "If

you are considering him, you should know his circumstances."

Her eyes grew wide. "I am certain he would prefer an heiress! I am of little standing — far too poor for the likes of him or you." She laughed bitterly. "Perhaps I should have accepted Mr. Collins when he offered."

Darcy whipped around. "Collins proposed to you? What was he thinking?"

Elizabeth gasped and drew back as if slapped. "I assure you, Mr. Darcy, that though I am unsuitable for you, I am not unacceptable to everyone." Tears began falling down her cheeks again.

Darcy shook his head and swallowed. "I did not mean you were unsuitable for him. He is not your equal, but it is not because of any deficiency in you. You are far superior to him." He dipped his head. "And to any lady of my acquaintance."

Elizabeth rose from the piano. "Stop it."

"Stop what?" he asked, concern etching his features.

"Speak your meaning."

"I am."

Elizabeth shook her head. "You said I was unacceptable because my portion was small, my family was ridiculous, and my relatives are in trade. Yet, you offer to reunite Jane and Mr. Bingley, and you dare to say I am superior to anyone? These things do not agree. Tell me which is true and which is false. What is your opinion of me?"

Darcy's stomach knotted. Had she heard him speaking to Richard? "When did I say you were unacceptable?"

Elizabeth turned away from him. It would be easier to admit where she had heard it if she did not have to see his face. "Yesterday. In the library."

"You heard that?"

His question was soft and anxious, causing her to turn toward him. "I did."

He closed his eyes and shook his head. Then, he crossed the room and taking her by her elbow led her to a seat. "I know that you may not believe me, but I said those things because I was jealous."

Elizabeth blinked. Of what was he jealous?

"You seemed to welcome Richard's attentions, and he seemed to be falling under your spell. I wished to dissuade him from pursuing you further."

Her head tipped, and her brows furrowed.

"Because it would be an embarrassment to your family?"

He shook his head and grasped her hands. "No, because I wanted you for myself."

Her eyes grew wide, and her lips parted. It was a charming expression and one that required he smile. "I admit that they are arguments I used in an attempt to discourage myself after I left Netherfield. And they worked well enough to keep me from climbing on my horse and returning to you as I wished to do each and every morning, but they have not discouraged me completely."

Her expression did not change except for a flutter of lashes. "I promised myself that if our paths should cross again without my arranging it, I would not leave you without pressing my suit as far as you would allow it." He smiled and squeezed her hands. "Each point of my arguments to myself can be reasoned away. What do I need with an heiress? My fortune is substantial, and my estate is not failing. Am I not already connected to trade through Bingley? Another connection would do little harm. And have you not met my aunt — we all have relations that are in one way or another ridiculous."

He released her hands and dared to lay a hand on her cheek. "I cannot speak more plainly than this. I love you, most ardently." He brushed a tear away with his thumb. "I would be honoured if you were to choose me as your husband, but I fear your opinion is such that it will never be." He drew a breath and removed his hand from her cheek. "And as much as it would pain me to see you with another, I would not place my wishes above yours."

Elizabeth stood and paced to the piano and back to the couch before returning to the piano and leaning on it as she turned to face him. "You love me?"

He nodded. "Most ardently."

"How?"

Darcy shrugged. "I do not know. I was in the middle of it before I knew I had begun." He waited as she considered what he had said, hoping against hope that he had some chance of winning her heart.

Chapter 7

Elizabeth drew and released a breath. Her brows furrowed. "You must be mistaken."

"I am not." His heart clenched. She was going to refuse him.

"But I am merely tolerable." She raised her shoulders and allowed them to fall. "You looked to find fault, did you not? Is that not why you wore such a serious and critical expression when at Netherfield?" Had she misunderstood his actions?

He stood and joined her at the piano. It was impossible to speak to her of his heart when she was so far from him. "I cannot explain away the first charge. I spoke harshly. There were reasons, but they do not justify my words. I was wrong. You have never ceased to tempt me. I found it challenging to conceal my interest. I wished to hear your thoughts, to see you smile, and to have you debate and challenge me, but there were others who would not allow it to pass unnoticed." He smiled sheepishly. "I spoke unkindly to those people in an effort to hide my feelings just as I scowled when I wished to worship."

Elizabeth laid a hand on her heart and reminded herself to breathe. He had not been critiquing and criticizing her every movement? "Miss Bingley holds no place in your heart?"

He chuckled. "Only as the sister of a friend because she must. I find her trying, at best."

Elizabeth tilted her head. Her brows were still furrowed. Was there anything she had accurately deciphered about Mr. Darcy?

"There is only you," he added, stepping just a half step closer to her.

She shook her head. "I do not know you." She gave a half shrug. "I thought I did, but I do not."

"What do you wish to know?" He clasped his hands behind his back to keep from touching her.

Her gaze dropped to the floor, and she shifted uneasily.

"You may ask anything."

She peeked up at him. "It does me no credit."

He smiled encouragingly. "That does not

signify. My actions have not done me a great service either."

"I...I....I was speaking with Miss de Bourgh." Her hands twisted nervously. "There were stories I had been told regarding you, but something she said has made me doubt their veracity."

Darcy's jaw clenched. He was nearly certain he knew the tales she had heard and from whom she had heard them. "Wickham."

It was only one word but spoken with such loathing that Elizabeth took a small step to the side.

Darcy drew in a great breath and released it slowly. "What did he tell you? That I refused him the living that he had previously rejected?"

She nodded as her brows furrowed. Wickham had told her about a living that was refused. He had not, however, mentioned having rejected it.

"Wickham is unfit for such a position, but that is not the sole reason for my refusal. Did he tell you that I had already given him three thousand pounds in lieu of the living and that he had wasted it in gambling and licentious living?" He briefly told her of his father's regard for Wickham.

Her eyes grew wide. "Three thousand pounds?"

"And the additional thousand my father had left

him, all gone within a very short time." He was certain there were other things that had been told in half-truths and veiled lies. "That is not the worst of it."

"It is not?" Darcy's expression was grim, and Elizabeth feared what else she might hear.

"He preyed upon my sister's tender heart."

Elizabeth gasped.

"Come. Sit. I will tell you the tale, but I must caution you that it is not pretty." He took a seat next to her on the couch and, gaining her assurance that what he shared would be heard in confidence, he began telling her about how Wickham had duped Georgiana into believing she was in love and about their planned elopement. "Had I not arrived when I did and had my sister's heart not been as soft as it is, she would have been lost to me."

"Is he truly so rapacious?" Elizabeth's emotions fluctuated between fury at Wickham's duplicity and disappointment in herself for accepting his tales so readily.

"He is." He could not resist taking her hand any longer. "He is also a practised deceiver, and not even I am capable of ferreting out every cheat. If I were, Mrs. Younge would have never been hired as my sister's companion, and Wickham's scheming would have come to naught before Georgiana was injured."

Elizabeth gave the hand that held hers a comforting squeeze. He was not as unreasonable as she had deemed him. Nor was he unable to acknowledge his own faults. "When did this happen?"

"Last summer."

She covered his hand with her free one. "It is your reason for speaking harshly." His sheepish smile and slight nod assured her that she was correct. She gave his hand a pat and then withdrawing both of her hands from his, she stood.

"Very well, Mr. Darcy. You are forgiven for your harsh words and grim looks." She cocked one brow impertinently. "I do hope you can forgive me for listening to such horrid tales and thinking so ill of you." She was rewarded with a smile. "I will take that as a yes. Now, where does that leave us?"

He cast a glance around the room as if puzzled and then with all seriousness replied, "I believe that leaves us locked in this sitting room."

Her eyes grew wide, and a small giggle escaped her. "You tease?"

"Though I am not as skilled at it as my cousin, I am capable of occasionally teasing, and contrary to the decrees of Miss Bingley, I am not averse to being teased by those I love." The way her lips pursed delightfully and her eyes sparkled, he was certain that he could learn to tease more often for such a reward.

Elizabeth turned and walked toward the window. He was not at all what she had thought. His character was noble and little wanting. His heart was soft and generous, and he was not without a sense of humor. He was very likely the exact sort of gentleman who would suit her best. "Besides your limited ability to tease, what else do you have to offer."

"Besides my heart?" He chuckled when she rolled her eyes and shook her head. "I have an estate and a sizeable income, but I think, you are already aware of that."

She nodded and leaned against the wall next to the window. "My mother may be silly and lacking in decorum, but I assure you that when it comes to a soiree or the eligibility of a gentleman, she is shrewd. I knew your status almost before I knew your name." She shrugged. "She has five daughters to see well-married." Her lips curled playfully. "My mother does not like you."

Darcy's hand flew to his chest, and his eyes questioned the truth of her statement.

"I am not her favourite, but even her least favourite daughter cannot be slighted without reproach." Elizabeth crossed her arms and lifted one shoulder in a half-shrug. "Your fortune, as well as your willingness to relieve her of a daughter — not to mention your seeing to the reunion of my sister and Mr. Bingley — will smooth any feathers you have ruffled. However, my father may not be so easily swayed. I am his favourite."

Darcy, who was crossing the room to her, stopped a few steps from his destination. "Are you accepting me?"

Elizabeth could not help the grin that spread across her face. A joyful bubbling was growing in her chest. "I am considering it."

He inclined his head in acknowledgment. He dared not completely hope that his greatest desire was nearly fulfilled. She could still change her mind, or her father could refuse. This thought caused his brows to furrow and a frown to form on his lips for a moment before a smile replaced it. "I have a library — two actually — one in town and another at Pemberley. They house thousands of books."

Her eyes grew wide again, and her lips parted slightly. "Thousands?"

He nodded. "They are all at your disposal, and your father's as well when he visits. There may even be a book or two with which I might be willing to part."

She shook her head and laughed. "A fortune for my mother and a book for my father — you, sir, are not without sense."

He stood directly before her. "What else must I do to convince you to accept me?" He placed his hands on her elbows and drew her a step closer to him. "All that I have is yours — body, mind, soul, and possessions."

"You will allow me to debate and read?"

He nodded. "With pleasure."

"You will not scold too often? I will make mistakes and act foolishly."

"I will attempt to be understanding."

She bit her lip and studied his face. "You will love me."

"With my dying breath. Will you love me?"

She nodded her head. "I think I will." Indeed, she felt she already might if the heady feeling of elation at his devotion to her was any indication.

"Will you marry me, whether or not we are discovered as we are?" He slid his hands up her arms to her shoulders and drew her even closer.

Darcy opened his mouth to continue speaking, but Elizabeth placed a finger on his lips. They were soft and warm, and for a moment she nearly forgot what she was going to say. She had never touched any man in such an intimate way. Her cheeks flushed, and she pulled her finger away. "I am not choosing you because I am forced to do so. I am choosing you because I wish to." Her heart fluttered at his smile and the look in his eyes.

Darcy cupped her face in his hands. "Thank you," he murmured before he kissed her. The touch of her lips against his nearly undid him. He wrapped an arm around her and pulled her close, pressing her to him.

Elizabeth did not resist. Instead, her arms found their way around his neck, and her fingers wove their way through his hair. So delicious was the sensation of him that she did not hear the door to the room open.

Mr. Collins stopped, frozen at the door. His mouth hung open but silent as if the words of greeting he had meant to share had been snatched from his throat. Richard nudged the poor shocked fellow from behind, causing the parson to take a stumbling step into the sitting room and freeing the rarely silent man's tongue.

"Cousin Elizabeth! What are you doing to poor Mr. Darcy? Unhand him at once!" Mr. Collins' voice broke through the haze in Elizabeth's mind, and her hands released their hold on Darcy. She attempted to pull away from him, but Darcy merely smiled and held her tightly.

"She is pleasing me — excessively." He smiled down at her and dropped a kiss on her forehead before loosening his hold. "She has done me the great honor of accepting my proposal," he continued.

"She has done what?" Mr. Collins, having found both the use of his tongue and his legs, had hurried across the room and stood next to Elizabeth, so that he was facing Darcy.

"She has agreed to be my wife."

Chapter 8

Richard leaned against the door frame, watching the scene before him unfold. He would interrupt if necessary, but for now, he was content to just observe. Anne stood beside him and would have entered the room, but his extended arm blocking her path and a shake of his head forestalled her.

Mr. Collins shifted his gaze from Darcy to Elizabeth and then back to Darcy once more before turning disapproving eyes on Elizabeth. "What have you done?"

The question was asked quietly, but, to Elizabeth, there was no mistaking Mr. Collin's displeasure. She was about to tell him that she had done nothing, but he was not pausing to allow it.

"Do you not know your place?" He took Elizabeth by the elbow and attempted to draw her away from Darcy. "Your father will have to be told, of course, but no one else need know. There is no need for a man such as Mr. Darcy to marry you. My mother has a sister in Edinburgh. You can go stay with her." He shook his head. "Trapping a man in his home. You are as wayward as your mother."

Darcy tightened his grip around Elizabeth's waist, pulling her towards him and away from Mr. Collins. "Mr. Collins!" The coldness of his voice caused Elizabeth to shiver, and Darcy paused for a moment to look down at her and smile. She was not the object of his displeasure, and he did not wish for her to feel as if she was. "Miss Elizabeth has not trapped me. I do not offer to marry her unwillingly or because of any imagined indiscretion." He waited for the flapping of Mr. Collins's lips to cease. "And you would do well not to speak of her mother in such a fashion." He smiled again at Elizabeth's upturned face. "It is entirely rude and unbecoming a man of your station."

Mr. Collins took a step towards Elizabeth, but a raised brow from Darcy halted him. Richard pushed off the door frame. Things were about to get ugly if there was not some sort of intervention. Darcy was wearing his nothing shall move this mountain expression, and Richard feared Collins was not bright enough to heed such a warning.

Richard gave his coat sleeves a tug to straighten them and, then, cleared his throat, drawing attention to his presence. He nodded to Darcy and Elizabeth before addressing Mr. Collins. "Was there a reason, sir, that you were seeking my cousin and yours?"

Mr. Collins looked blankly from Richard to Darcy and back again. Richard shook his head and sighed. How his aunt had managed to select this buffoon as her parson was beyond him! "I believe you mentioned tea when I met you in the hall."

Mr. Collins blinked. "Yes, yes, that is correct. Lady Catherine had asked me to tell Cousin Elizabeth that her presence was required." He turned to Elizabeth, a dour expression on his face. "Come along. One mustn't keep Lady Catherine waiting."

Anne stepped around Richard. "I will see that Miss Bennet finds the correct room."

"But it is my duty –"

"You would deny me?"

Anne's voice was so full of indignation and sounded so much like her mother's that Richard had to cough to cover a laugh. He could tell by the slight upward tilt of her lips that she also found amusement in the current proceedings.

"My mother would be distressed to hear such a thing. I am certain she would be much better pleased if you were to tell her that I requested the privilege of escorting our guest to tea and you, knowing your place,"–Richard saw her lips twitch as she attempted to keep her features serious–"thought it best to oblige me."

"But my cousin..." Mr. Collins looked at Elizabeth.

"Is there something wrong with your cousin?" asked Anne, tipping her head and studying Elizabeth before turning wide questioning eyes at Mr. Collins. "She looks well to me. My cousin, on the other hand, could use some work."

Richard could not help the laugh that escaped him at that comment. "I shall see to our cousin," he said to Anne, "if you will see to Miss Bennet." He gave Mr. Collins a firm stare and tilted his head toward the door. "You will tell my aunt we will join her shortly." He kept his intent gaze on the parson until the man decided it was best to do as instructed.

"Miss Bennet." Anne extended a hand.

Reluctantly, Darcy released Elizabeth from his embrace, though his hand lingered on hers.

"I will see that she is safe," Anne assured him.

Darcy gave a small smile and nod in response, but he still seemed reluctant to let her go.

Was he worried for her safety? The thought felt strange to Elizabeth. She could not help but compare such a response to that of her father who would have gladly allowed Elizabeth to follow after Collins for the sole purpose of seeing what might follow. Oh, her father would not allow her to fall into an untenable situation — she knew this for a certainty. Had he not allowed her to refuse Mr. Collins's offer of marriage? But he would also not watch with the intent to protect nearly as much as the hope of finding something over which to laugh later. Was that perhaps why her father had allowed Mr. Collins to present his suit at all? She placed her hand in Miss de Bourgh's and allowed herself to be led from the room.

She had never truly considered this a fault in her father before now, and the realization was rather unsettling. She turned her head to look back to the sitting room door. "Mr. Darcy is a very good man, is he not?" Quite a bit better than she had ever imagined. Indeed, she was swiftly coming to the conclusion that there were few men who were superior to Mr. Darcy in character.

"Without question," Anne agreed.

"He is not what I thought. I have been completely wrong about him." Elizabeth finally admitted aloud the thought that had been beginning to form in her mind from the moment Mr. Darcy entered the parsonage two days ago.

"How have you been wrong?" Anne asked as they descended the stairs.

"I thought him arrogant."

"He is proud," said Anne.

"But not improperly so. There is a pride of position, but not of one who lords that position over another solely for the sake of making them feel inferior." Elizabeth stopped on a stair about halfway down the grand staircase and turned to look back up from where they had come.

Anne released Elizabeth's hand and leaned against the balustrades across from her. "His countenance is so often grave when amongst strangers or those who make him feel ill at ease."

Elizabeth nodded. "He scrutinizes."

Anne laughed. "That he does!"

"But he is wise and discerning, is he not" Elizabeth turned questioning eyes towards Anne. There were still things that she did not know about the man to whom she had pledged her life. She once again wished for her sister Jane to be here to help her arrange her muddled thoughts

"I would say he is, but not always. He is not without fault. There is the matter of his sister," she said the last part quietly.

Elizabeth's brows furrowed as she thought about what she had learned of Georgiana's narrow escape from Wickham. Mr. Darcy had readily admitted to having been duped by Mrs. Younge and to being less attentive than perhaps he should have been. He did not glance over it or deny any part he may have played in the affair. In fact, she had a distinct feeling that he felt his error far more heavily than he should.

Again, she was struck by the contrast between Mr. Darcy and her father. Her father would have found that the greatest part of the story lay with the foolishness of the young lady in being so easily led by pretty words and a pleasing countenance. Did he not speak of her younger sisters in such a fashion? Were their follies not his responsibility? Should he not be correcting them and their mother? Yet, he only found amusement. If he disapproved, he said very little! She shook her head. "Mr. Darcy is not without fault, and he accepts that he is not." A small smile touched her lips as she once again realized just how fine a gentleman Mr. Darcy was.

Anne took a step down the staircase, and Elizabeth followed. "Was it only his pride that you had gotten wrong?"

Elizabeth shook her head. "I had formed a great many incorrect notions about him, but they were all based on my thinking him arrogant." She paused for a moment on the second step from the bottom. Her mind travelled back up to the room with the piano and the man she had discovered there.

"If he had not wounded my vanity, my vision of his character might have been more clear." She had been so determined to not like him and find fault. Her sister and even her own conscience told her she might be wrong. She shook her head and descended the last two steps. Indeed, that was the reason she had not been able to decipher his character — her conscience would not allow it. Her doubts had suggested she might be judging unfairly. Now, there were no doubts to cloud her appraisal of the man. She felt as if a veil had been lifted.

"So you are happy to be tied to him?"

Elizabeth's eyes grew wide, and her brows rose as she realized that she was indeed happy to be tied to Mr. Darcy. She nodded as a smile spread across her face. She was happy, but it was more than that: her soul felt at peace. There was no indecision, no wavering, not a morsel of regret. Marrying Mr. Darcy was right, and not just because she had been found with him in a compromising position.

"Then, I am happy that all has worked out as it should," said Anne with a smile as she led Elizabeth into her mother's sitting room.

Chapter 9

Elizabeth was happy to see Charlotte was also at Rosings. Mr. Collins was deep in whispered discussion with Lady Catherine as Elizabeth and Anne entered the room and took a seat near Mrs. Collins.

"What has happened?" Charlotte whispered. "My husband was in quite a state when he entered and went directly to Lady Catherine and began whispering to her. Was there an issue with your practising. You did practise, did you not" Charlotte cast a second wary glance toward her husband as she spoke in hushed tones.

Elizabeth could not contain her smile. "I am to marry," she said, keeping her voice low.

Charlotte's eyes grew wide. "Whom?" her lips formed the word, but no sound accompanied it.

"Oh, Charlotte," Elizabeth said, grasping one of

her friend's hands. "I have been so wrong, and you have been so right. He loves me, Charlotte, just as you claimed."

Charlotte's eyes stayed wide, and her mouth dropped open before forming a smile. "Mr. Darcy?" she whispered.

Elizabeth nodded her head.

"But you are smiling. I thought you did not like him."

Elizabeth touched her lips with the tips of her fingers. "It is the strangest thing."

Charlotte caught a small laugh before it could draw her husband's attention. "You are happy?"

Again, Elizabeth nodded. "It is the strangest thing," she repeated.

"But my husband is not," Charlotte added with a raised brow.

"They were discovered together in the room with the piano," Anne added the hushed explanation. "Kissing."

Charlotte's eyes were again wide and wary as she looked from Elizabeth to her husband.

"Mr. Darcy was not fully dressed," Anne added.

Elizabeth's mouth dropped open at Anne's comment.

"He was not," Elizabeth looked toward Lady Catherine and then back to Charlotte and added, "undressed," in as low a whisper as she could manage. "At least not then."

Charlotte was about to ask for a further explanation of the comment, but Lady Catherine chose that moment to intervene.

"Miss Bennet."

"Yes, my lady," Elizabeth replied, squeezing Charlotte's hand. She could tell by the way Lady Catherine's chin was raised and how she peered down her nose at Elizabeth that she was not pleased.

"A troubling account has reached me. It seems you did not use your full practice time to improve your skills at the piano. Was the instrument not to your liking?"

Elizabeth blinked. This was not the accusation she had anticipated, and from the opening and closing of Mr. Collins's mouth, it was not the accusation he expected either.

"No, my lady, I did not use the full time to practice," she replied. "There were distractions."

Mr. Collins could not contain himself any longer and harrumphed softly.

"Was one of these distractions my nephew?" Lady Catherine plucked at the lace at her wrist.

"Yes, my lady, Mr. Darcy was one distraction." Elizabeth could feel her face growing warm.

Lady Catherine's eyes stayed lowered as she seemed intent on straightening that bit of lace. "Did you seduce him?"

Elizabeth gasped.

Lady Catherine's lips twitched briefly before she raised her gaze to take in the look of shock on Elizabeth's face.

"No, my lady. I did not."

Lady Catherine's left shoulder rose and fell. "Mr. Collins fears you did."

Elizabeth shook her head. "I did not."

Lady Catherine's smile was soft. She could see that Elizabeth was on the verge of tears at having been accused of such an unseemly thing. It was a credit to the lady's honor to be so shaken by such claims. "Then perhaps you can tell me how you came to be embracing my nephew when Mr. Collins entered the locked music room."

Again, Elizabeth gasped. "I...I... did not lock the door," she stammered.

Lady Catherine merely smiled and waited while Mr. Collins barely contained a comment.

Elizabeth swallowed. "I was on my way to practice, and Colonel Fitzwilliam, who had offered to escort me to the correct room, had to tend to some matter of business. He told me that the room I sought was three doors up on the left from where we stood, so that is where I went. I entered and closed the door." Elizabeth paused, and her brows furrowed. The door had not been locked when she entered and yet when she had turned to leave moments later it was. "It was not the correct room, but I could not leave." She shook her head. "It is most odd. A door cannot lock itself, can it?"

Lady Catherine shrugged. "None at Rosings do."

"Then how was it locked after I entered if I did not lock it?" She thought back to when she closed the door. It had made two latching sounds. She had not thought much of it at the time, but now it struck her as not right.

"I could not say," said Lady Catherine, plucking at the lace on her other sleeve. "You say you were in the wrong room, but Mr. Collins discovered you in the correct room. How did that come to be?"

"There is a door that connects Mr. Darcy's room to the sitting room between his room and the one Miss Darcy uses when she visits," said Elizabeth. "That room's door was also locked." Her head tipped as she considered that fact. "I was so mortified at having seen Mr. Darcy in his dressing gown and having spoken to him so harshly that I did not stop to consider how I was to enter that room to practice if the door was locked."

"Mr. Darcy was in his dressing gown?" Mr. Collins asked in surprise.

Elizabeth nodded. "I believe he had just exited his bath. His hair was wet." Though she was sharing what had happened, her mind was not fully thinking about what she was saying. It was still trying to reason away the locked doors.

She gasped almost in unison with Charlotte, who had been shocked by Elizabeth's revelation about Mr. Darcy and his bath.

"Someone locked it!" Elizabeth exclaimed. "Someone wished me to be locked in that room with Mr. Darcy." She turned toward Anne. "Do you know who?" she asked.

"I do," said Darcy, entering the room.

"It is good to see you properly dressed," said

Lady Catherine. "Miss Elizabeth was just telling me how you were in a robe when she entered your bedroom, and Mr. Collins assures me that you were not wearing boots or a coat when he discovered you and Miss Elizabeth in a most compromising position."

Darcy tugged Richard forward and then gave him a shove toward a chair. "Richard would like to say something to you," he said, turning to Elizabeth.

Richard sank into the chair that Darcy had indicated he take. Darcy had not been pleased to find out the truth of what had happened. He had not raised more than his voice at Richard, but he had made certain that Richard knew there would be a price to pay if he did not apologize to Elizabeth for his part in the scheme. Richard swallowed and bowed his head slightly. "I am to apologize for directing you to the wrong room."

"And?" Darcy prodded.

Richard grimaced. "And locking the door."

Elizabeth's lips parted in surprise, and Mr. Collins sputtered something unintelligible.

"I will not, however, apologize for the results."

Richard leaned back, folded his arms across his chest, and gave Darcy a defiant glare.

"She cannot marry him," sputtered Mr. Collins. "This must be stopped."

"Why?" asked Lady Catherine.

"Why?" repeated Mr. Collins. "Why?" he repeated a second time. He flapped his arm in Elizabeth's direction. "She is beneath him. Her connections are not so great as his."

"I do not see why that signifies," said Lady Catherine. "All I have learned of Miss Bennet is satisfactory to me. Her father is a gentleman with an estate that has been in the family's possession for three generations. She is a lady of exceptional character. She is not a diamond of the first waters, but she is pretty. Her mind, I understand, is lively, and though she is without refinement in her accomplishments, she is not devoid of them."

"But what of Miss de Bourgh?" Mr. Collins protested.

Lady Catherine blinked and looked at Anne and then back to Mr. Collins. "What of my daughter?"

"Is she not betrothed to Mr. Darcy?"

Darcy chuckled. "I have never offered, nor do I intend to make an offer."

A smile spread across Lady Catherine's face. "And I would have never accepted his offer if he made it."

"You would not?" Darcy asked in surprise. "I thought you wished it."

Lady Catherine rose from her chair. "I let you think that. It made it easier to search for the right lady if you thought I would be displeased should you tell me you were not marrying Anne." She nodded her thanks for the tea tray that had been set up and began to pour. "Did I not do a good job of finding a lady for you?" she asked as she lifted a cup of tea for Anne to pass to one of their guests.

Darcy's mouth hung open.

"Anne is too delicate for a northern climate," said Lady Catherine as she poured another cup of tea. "And I really could not bear to have her so far from me." She handed the cup to Anne. "And what would poor Mr. Abney do if you stole Anne away from Kent. He would never marry, and that would be a shame to have his estate untouched by a feminine hand."

Darcy shook his head. "Mr. Abney?"

Lady Catherine nodded. "He has made his

overtures." Anne blushed and smiled as she took a third cup from her mother.

"When I heard about Miss Bennet's refusal of Mr. Collins and her seeming dislike of you," Lady Catherine continued, "I knew she was the one."

Darcy's brows furrowed, and he looked at his aunt and then Elizabeth, who was listening intently but looking as bemused as he felt. "You chose Miss Bennet because she did not like me?"

Lady Catherine smiled and shook her head. "No, because she was intelligent and given to debate. She did not dislike you."

Darcy opened his mouth and then clamped it shut again. His aunt was making very little sense.

"You were rude," said Lady Catherine, "and any lady worth her salt and able to take her place in this family would not let such a thing pass without displeasure." She shook her head gently and chuckled. "Miss Bennet did not shun you. She engaged in a battle of wits, proving her value to you. And you were enchanted."

"But she did not like me."

"No, I did not," said Elizabeth.

Lady Catherine smiled. "A misunderstanding. That is all it was." She handed Darcy a cup of tea and patted his cheek. "How could anyone dislike you once they got to know you?" She returned to pour her own cup of tea. "That is why you had to be forced to spend time together. So, Miss Bennet could come to know and love you as Anne, Richard, and I do." She turned to Mr. Collins. "I am afraid you will have to accept that fact that you were instrumental in bringing such joy to my family."

Mr. Collins nodded mutely and slumped into a chair, clearly not feeling quite the thing.

Chapter 10

Mr. Collins remained melancholy for a full three days, only cheering up enough to do a credible job of playing the part of a carefree parson as required for services. On the third day, after he had finished his duties at the church, he seemed to have resolved whatever matter was causing him discomfort and, unfortunately for Elizabeth, found his tongue. Many were the comments about propriety and the recommendations of books that should and should not be read by ladies who aspired to such lofty positions as the niece of an earl. He could not stress to her just how important it was that she do her best to secure the Bennet family name as one worthy of consideration for positions of honor.

"And your sisters," he said as the party from the parsonage walked to Rosings to spend the evening with Lady Catherine, "they could benefit from some instruction. It is not outside the realm of possibility that your mother would insist upon at least one of them attending a school if it meant the possibility of an excellent match. Why, with the name of Fitzwilliam and Darcy attached to her relations, she would be worthy of perhaps a baronet's notice even without a fortune to her name. Connections, you see, are quite valuable."

"Mr. Collins," Charlotte said in a low voice. "It is not for us to arrange the disposal of all Elizabeth's sisters."

He harrumphed. "Her father has done a poor job of it thus far. He thinks them capable of selecting their own match, yet he does not present them in a greater society than Meryton. A shabby job he has done," he muttered, "a right shabby job."

"Mr. Collins," Charlotte's voice remained soft but had taken on an edge. "I begin to think you unhappily married."

This comment brought an abrupt stop to the progress of the group.

Elizabeth and Maria drew back a short distance

to give a perceived amount of privacy to the couple.

"My dear," said Mr. Collins. "Mr. Bennet's best decision was to allow his daughter to refuse me." He patted his wife's hand and drew her a step closer to him. "You are my blessing." He lifted her hand and gave it a kiss.

Elizabeth's mouth dropped open slightly as she saw her friend duck her head and blush.

"Very well, you are forgiven for your foul mood," said Charlotte. "Do not fear about your cousins getting married. I am certain that they will all eventually find a home. They are far too pretty to be left sitting on the shelf. And do not forget that having friends with such connections will do my sister no harm."

"Ah, you are wise," Mr. Collins muttered as he resumed walking. "Yes, yes. I had thought this arrangement to be a potential disaster, but perhaps I have been seeing it from the wrong perspective. It is perhaps the benevolence of the Lord Almighty being poured out on his servant."

"Indeed, it might be," said Charlotte.

The remainder of the walk was made in silence as Mr. Collins waxed eloquent on the many unusual working of Providence in setting His good and proper plans into action. They had nearly reached the steps at Rosings when he was finally reaching the end of his circle through the many acts of God in ordering and directing his children.

"And we must remember that it was a harlot who was used to shelter Joshua and Caleb, and even the mighty King David stumbled." He nodded in agreement with himself as he continued the thought. "Therefore, it is not unthinkable that He should also use a wayward cousin to bring great blessing to our family."

"Mr. Collins!" Charlotte removed her hand from his arm. "I will not listen to you speak of Elizabeth or Mr. Darcy in such a fashion. As has been explained previously, Elizabeth was led astray by Colonel Fitzwilliam and locked — trapped — in that room with Mr. Darcy. She did not plot to capture him." She lowered her voice. "And there was no seduction."

Mr. Collins shrugged. "Perhaps, but it was still highly improper for her to be kissing him, and in such a fashion!"

"Very well, Mr. Collins, I will allow that kissing might not have been proper. However, I do think

I remember someone kissing me when I had agreed to marry him, and I dare say hypocrisy is not becoming."

Mr. Collins's eyes grew wide, and his face became quite red. "I shall remember that," he muttered. Then, turning to Elizabeth, he added, "You are forgiven your folly." Before Elizabeth could respond, he was up the steps and knocking at the door.

Charlotte stepped closer to Elizabeth and Maria. "All will be well now. He will write his pleasure at your good fortune to your father," she flicked her brows up quickly, "without any mention of impropriety. One must always know how to guide her husband if he seems to be going astray." She winked and turned to follow her husband into Rosings.

And all was well, or as well as one might expect with a man such as Mr. Collins. It appeared from the way he sought out Mr. Darcy to praise him that evening and the flattering comments he made about Elizabeth that both she and Mr. Darcy had been restored in his good opinion. However, the colonel did not fare so well. He was watched with suspicion.

That night, upon returning to the parsonage, Mr. Collins sat down and wrote a most satisfactory letter to Mr. Bennet, declaring the joyful news that Elizabeth's father should expect a call from a particular gentleman for a very specific purpose.

It was, therefore, a rather peaceful week in Kent, both at the parsonage and Rosings, that followed the passing of Easter. Elizabeth found a book of sermons near her place in the breakfast room each morning, open to what Mr. Collins thought to be an appropriate lesson on some matter of female duty.

This morning was no different. Elizabeth smiled and nodded to her cousins and allowed her eyes to skim over the contents of the lesson enough to satisfy Mr. Collins, so he felt secure in leaving her to complete the task on her own. She made certain to read a few passages so that when questioned later, she might be able to respond with some semblance of knowledge on the matter.

"He wishes you to do well," Charlotte assured her. "Being a wife, and if the Lord sees fit, a mother is not a small task, though having your own home is such a pleasant thing."

Elizabeth smiled as Charlotte sighed and sank

back in her chair. Having a modest home of her own had always been Charlotte's aim in life, and Elizabeth was happy to see her friend so well settled.

"I was right about him, was I not?" Charlotte's eyes twinkled over the rim of her cup as she took a sip of tea. "He was in love with you."

Elizabeth's cheeks grew warm. Mr. Darcy being in love with her was still such a novel idea, but it was one that was quickly settling into her reality and becoming a piece of her.

"When does he ride to Longbourn to speak to your father?" Charlotte placed her cup on the table and broke off a piece of a roll and spread it with butter.

"Tomorrow, if the weather holds," Elizabeth replied, closing the book of sermons and turning her attention to her own breakfast. A strange uneasiness settled in around her. It had been happening each time she spoke about Mr. Darcy's trip to call on her father. She took a small sip of her tea. She was nervous about her father's reception of the request, but this unsettled feeling seemed to be in addition to that flutter of nerves.

"I wonder if I should not travel with him," she

said. "My father will wonder at my reversal of opinion. He may wish to speak with me before he grants his approval."

Charlotte's brows flicked upward, and she smiled knowingly. "A letter should suffice."

Elizabeth shook her head. "He may have questions that I have not thought to answer."

"You not think of the answers to your father's questions before he asks them?" Charlotte tsked and shook her head. "Not likely, my dear."

Elizabeth knew this to be true. She was quite good at knowing just how her father would think about something, yet writing a letter did not ease her spirit the way the idea of travelling with Mr. Darcy did.

"I have never accepted a proposal of marriage before, so I cannot predict what he will wish to know," she protested weakly.

Charlotte shrugged and sighed. "Go with him if you must, but do be honest about your reasons." She stood and came round the table to give the top of Elizabeth's head a kiss. "You wish to go with him because you do not wish to be parted from him."

Elizabeth gasped and would have retorted that

what Charlotte said was untrue, except for two facts, one, Charlotte had already left the room and two, Elizabeth's heart spoke to her of her friend's wisdom.

Elizabeth was still thinking about Charlotte's comment about not wishing to be parted from Mr. Darcy when she went to fetch her hat for her walk in the grove. She could not come to an acceptable reason for her wish to be with him. She knew she enjoyed his presence. However, she also enjoyed the presence of Colonel Fitzwilliam, yet when she considered Colonel Fitzwilliam's departure from Kent, she felt no great disappointment. It was the strangest thing — Elizabeth stopped mid-thought and mid-descent of the stairs as a familiar voice was heard in the sitting room. Her father was here?

"I do apologize for arriving without warning."

"It is no imposition, Mr. Bennet." Elizabeth heard Charlotte assuring him.

"My wife would have me search out the full extent of the matter about which your husband wrote. I must admit that it has taken us by surprise."

Elizabeth placed her bonnet on the table in the

foyer and, instead of going outside, turned into the sitting room. "Papa."

A smile of delight lit Mr. Bennet's eyes as he turned to greet her. "Ah, my Lizzy, you are a welcome sight."

Elizabeth gave him a hug and took a seat near Charlotte. "What brings you to Kent? All is well at Longbourn, I hope. Mama and my sisters are all well?"

"As well as can be expected after the news I received from Mr. Collins." Her father's head tipped, and his brows rose in question. "Your mother insisted that I come see you. She will not be settled until she knows all, and I shall have no peace until she is settled." He chuckled and crossed his ankles as he leaned back and peered at Elizabeth, who was doing her best to look calm despite the rapid rhythm of her heart.

"Am I to understand that you have grown fond enough of Mr. Darcy to accept an offer of marriage?"

Elizabeth nodded slowly. "I have."

Mr. Bennet blinked. "Well, well, well. So it is as Sir William suspected. The gentleman was fascinated by you."

Elizabeth's cheeks grew warm.

"He is wealthy. You will have no fear of want," he paused, "but wealth has never been your desire."

It was true, though Elizabeth wished for a home with ample income to be comfortable, she had never sought riches in a marriage partner. She had avowed that she would not marry unless it was to a man whom she could respect and would respect her in turn, nor would she be induced into matrimony without the deepest of affection. "It is still not my desire," she admitted.

Mr. Bennet's brows rose, and he clasped his hands in front of his stomach. "Then my daughter, you must explain yourself to me."

Elizabeth's brows furrowed. How was she supposed to explain something that she, herself, did not fully comprehend?

"Surely, my Lizzy, there must be a reason for your reversal of opinion of the man. Do you not still find him proud?" Her father asked as he carefully watched her face.

"Not improperly so," said Elizabeth. "I admit that I did find him to be arrogant." She sighed.

"His words at the assembly hurt me, and I allowed them to colour my judgment of him. "

Mr. Bennet nodded. "That is not unusual."

"But it is not right," protested Elizabeth. "I listened to stories about Mr. Darcy and delighted to hear him spoken of in unflattering ways. Those stories — by a man who should not be trusted –" she looked pointedly at her father, "those stories fed my dislike. They satisfied me not because I found them credible, for I did not stop to consider their veracity. They satisfied me because they agreed with my judgment based on a few hurtful comments. I did not bother to look for anything but fault in Mr. Darcy's character. My wounded pride would not allow me to see anything different from what I wished to see."

Mr. Bennet's lips curled in amusement as his daughter's voice became stronger and more forceful in her defence of her opinions being wrong.

Elizabeth stood and paced the floor behind the sofa on which she had been sitting. "The things that were told to me by Mr. Wickham were half-truths at best. He has not been ill-treated by Mr.

Darcy. In fact, it is Mr. Darcy who has suffered at the schemes of Mr. Wickham."

Mr. Bennet's brows rose. "Indeed?"

"I cannot tell you all, for I have promised I would not." She stopped and mentally shuffled through what she now knew of Wickham searching for something to tell her father that would not violate her promise but would allow her father to see Wickham for what he was. "Do you remember how Mr. Wickham claimed that Mr. Darcy refused to give him a living?"

Mr. Bennet nodded. "It was a request of Mr. Darcy's father to bestow it."

"It was," Elizabeth came around the sofa and sat on the edge of it, facing her father. "It was not Mr. Darcy who refused but rather Mr. Wickham. He did not wish to take orders, and so Mr. Darcy paid Mr. Wickham a sizeable sum in lieu of the living. It was not until Mr. Wickham had wasted all the money and came back hoping to claim the living that Mr. Darcy refused to give it to him." She leaned forward towards her father. "Three thousand pound along with an additional thousand given to Mr. Wickham by Mr. Darcy's father was gone within three years. Four thousand pounds." She shook her head. The fact that so much had been wasted on frivolous living still shocked her.

"So much?" Mr. Bennet could not hide his surprise.

Elizabeth nodded. "There is more, but I cannot speak of it." She sighed. "You would do well to keep my sisters away from him."

Mr. Bennet's brows rose even higher, and his eyes grew wider. "Indeed?"

Elizabeth nodded. "Once I knew of the foolishness of my trusting Mr. Wickham, I had to reconsider my assessment of Mr. Darcy." She sighed, and her lips curled into a small smile. "I was so utterly wrong about him, Papa. He is not what we thought. He is a caring brother, cousin, nephew, and friend. He is wise, but not without fault, which he will readily admit. When he errs, he makes amends. " Her head tilted as she thought. "He is of noble character, Papa, and he promises not to scold too often when I make mistakes and wishes for me to read and debate. He does not find my wit to be a detriment." Her smile grew. "And, Papa," she clasped his hands, "he has thousands of books in his libraries." She tucked her lower lip between her teeth.

"Thousands?" Mr. Bennet blinked at the thought.

"Yes, Papa, and all at our disposal."

It was a moment before Mr. Bennet's brows drew together and his eyes twinkled with delight. "So you would marry him for his libraries?"

She shook her head and laughed. "No, Papa, but Mr. Darcy thought it might help you grant your blessing."

Mr. Bennet chuckled. "He respects you?"

Elizabeth nodded.

"Does he love you?" Mr. Bennet's eyes grew serious.

Elizabeth nodded again. "Most ardently."

Mr. Bennet sighed. "I have heard in your speech that you respect him."

Elizabeth nodded slowly. "Very much."

"Do you love him?"

Elizabeth's brows drew together, and her shoulders lifted and lowered as she shook her head. "I do not know. I think, I might."

Mr. Bennet grasped her hands firmly. "My daughter, if I were to refuse you this request, and

Mr. Darcy were to return to Derbyshire never to return, what would you do?"

Elizabeth shook her head in disbelief. Her mouth opened, and she closed it as if she were lost for words. Her heart ached, and her chest constricted, making it hard to breathe.

Mr. Bennet released her hands and searched for his handkerchief, so that she could dry her tears. "Would you wish to follow him?" he asked softly.

She nodded.

Mr. Bennet's smile was soft, as were his words. "You love him. I am satisfied." He blinked against his own unshed tears, and then with a sigh, he clapped his hands on the arms of his chair and pushed to his feet. "Now, where might I find the man who has had the audacity to steal my Lizzy's heart, so that I might give him my permission to continue to care for it?"

Chapter 11

Mr. Bennet found his quarry in the grove, pacing beneath a large tree and swatting at the grass with his walking stick. Once Darcy got over his shock at coming face to face with Elizabeth's father so unexpectedly, he did an admirable job in presenting his request. Mr. Bennet wished to discomfit the man, but as he watched Darcy wring the life from his hat, he relented and readily gave his permission.

"I will require some time to come to terms with losing my daughter, and my wife will wish to make her good fortune known far and wide," Mr. Bennet watched the tip of his walking stick as he twirled it in a circle. "A month should suffice. Although I would wish for longer, it is doubtful that you, Lizzy, or I could tolerate Mrs. Bennet's raptures for any longer than a month." He cradled his stick in his arms much as he did his rifle when out on a hunt. "Will Mr. Bingley be returning to Netherfield, or do you require accommodations at Longbourn?"

Darcy thought there was a bit of an accusatory tone to Mr. Bennet's question. It seemed that it was not only Elizabeth who held him responsible for Bingley's departure. "I am uncertain, but I believe he may indeed return. The outcome of his calling at the Gardiners will be the deciding factor."

Mr. Bennet's brows rose. "He has gone to call at the Gardiners? I had not heard such. Jane is circumspect, but I would think she would have mentioned seeing a friend such as Mr. Bingley in one of her letters."

"He has only just received notice of Miss Bennet being in town," said Darcy. "I have not had a reply, nor has Miss Elizabeth had word from her sister, so I am uncertain if the call has taken place or the results." He turned to Mr. Bennet. "Had I known Miss Bennet was in town or that she had called on Bingley's sisters, I would have informed Mr. Bingley of her presence much sooner. However,

I only just discovered this information when I arrived in Kent."

Mr. Bennet's lips puckered and relaxed as his brows drew together in question.

Darcy shifted uneasily under the man's scrutiny. "When we left Netherfield, I thought Miss Bennet indifferent and cautioned my friend against forming too deep an attachment." He sighed. "Miss Elizabeth assures me I was wrong." He grimaced. "And from the melancholy I have observed in my friend, my warning came too late as it was."

One corner of Mr. Bennet's mouth tipped upwards in a half smile. "So my wife's raptures might not be confined only to Elizabeth's conquest of a wealthy gentleman?"

Darcy shook his head and chuckled slightly. "Mrs. Bennet might be doubly delighted, but I cannot guarantee it."

"Very good. Very good, indeed." Mr. Bennet's smile grew wide. "I must request one more thing of you for my wife's sake."

"Whatever you wish," said Darcy.

Mr. Bennet smirked. "I could be requesting something very nearly impossible."

"Whatever you ask, if it is in my power to provide it, I will," Darcy assured him.

Mr. Bennet's smile softened, and Darcy was surprised to see understanding in the gentleman's eyes. "You love my Lizzy dearly, do you not?"

Darcy felt his ears and cheeks grow warm. He had admitted his love for Elizabeth to Elizabeth and even to his aunt and cousins without much uneasiness, but admitting it to her father was somewhat more disquieting. "More than life itself, sir," he answered softly.

Mr. Bennet swallowed and blinked against the tears that wished to fall. It was all for which he had wished for his Lizzy — to be loved completely. "For some of us, such a thing is not easily admitted." He looked behind him down the path he had taken from the parsonage. "She is special to me — in a way her sisters are not, so it does my heart good to hear she will be loved as she deserves. It is still not easy to part with her, of course."

"I shall likely feel the same when I have to part with my sister."

Mr. Bennet nodded slowly. "You wish for their happiness, you know."

"I do."

Mr. Bennet stood silently for a moment longer before turning around and continuing on his walk with Mr. Darcy. "To my request," he began, "my wife would be greatly pleased if you were to marry by special license."

This request was speedily agreed to, and Mr. Bennet was petitioned that, after her time in Kent was up, Elizabeth be allowed to stay longer in town than first planned. There was a need to introduce Elizabeth not only to his sister but also to his uncle, Lord Matlock.

As Mr. Bennet saw it, it was wise for both Darcy and Elizabeth to know if their marriage would meet with approbation or displeasure while they were still preparing for life as a married couple, and so he agreed. He would stop at Gardiner's on his return to Longbourn and inform them of the change and the reason.

And so it transpired that after Darcy's time in Kent was at an end, he returned to London to share the news of his betrothal with his sister and his uncle.

Shortly thereafter, Elizabeth joined him in town for a grand dinner party in her honor. So grand was this party, and so happy the occasion, it necessitated the presence of Lady Catherine and Anne. The Gardiners were also invited as were Mr. Bingley and Jane. Fortunately, the week prior to this soiree, indeed before the invitations had arrived, the Hursts, with Caroline in tow, had removed to a small estate in the country to visit a friend with a cousin of marriageable age and fortune.

Therefore, it was a companionable group that met that evening at Darcy House. The dining room was set with its finest and not a surface that could hold a shine was dim. All was to be presented at its best for the new mistress.

"What do you think of Darcy House?" Darcy asked Elizabeth as they slipped out the door to the terrace.

"It is very grand." Elizabeth turned to look at the house from the bottom of the garden steps. "It is beautiful." She smiled and chuckled. "I fear I will not do it justice, for I am merely tolerable, and it is so handsome." She turned laughing eyes toward Darcy.

Over the days they had spent at Rosings, they had fallen into an easy friendship. It had started that afternoon in the music room when the blinders of prejudice had been removed, and it had continued through each walk in the groves, ride in the countryside, and afternoon and evening spent in each other's company.

Elizabeth had found Darcy to be a person with whom she could share a great camaraderie. They had discussed a great number of topics, from preferences of seasons and plants, to books and politics, to family and dreams and wishes for the future. Not every topic had been delved into with any degree of depth as to think it thoroughly canvassed, but it had been touched in such a way as to assure the pair that they were indeed companionably matched. That is not to say, of course, that either one or the other would not on some point or another be unwilling to shift their opinion, but on the important matters of life and love, they were in almost unanimous agreement.

Darcy shook his head and, taking her hand, lead her down a path away from the room filled with people and the few who were enjoying the coolness of evening on the terrace. "Will you ever forget those words?"

"It is unlikely," she said with a laugh.

"They are untrue, you know." He pulled her close to his side. "You are definitely handsome enough to tempt me," he leaned closer to her ear and added in a whisper, "beyond reason." It was a statement he had proven with ardent kisses at least once per day while at Rosings.

Elizabeth blushed and ducked her head. She was still not entirely at ease with this new, complimentary Mr. Darcy. Parrying and dodging quips, refuting arguments, and challenging ideas were Elizabeth's natural bent when it came to engaging others in conversation. Having to speak of one's inner desires and feelings was more challenging, but it was something to which she was slowly growing accustomed. For all of her life, there had only been one person with whom she shared such thoughts — Jane, but now that role would be filled, as it had been during the last portion of her stay in Kent, by Mr. Darcy — her husband. That word — husband — made her stomach flop and a skitter of delight race up her spine.

"Have I silenced you?" There was laughter in Darcy's tone.

"I am afraid you have," said Elizabeth, glancing up at him and giving him a small smile.

Husband, she said the word once more in her mind, and the excited delight of a moment ago slid into a welcome comforting feeling that wrapped around her heart tightly. How she had ever doubted it was love for the man beside her that longed for his presence and good opinion, she was unsure. It was stubbornness, she supposed, or naivety, or just plain fear of the heretofore unfamiliar.

She had never been in love. It was not something which had been explained in books or described with adequacy by any friend or relation. She credited this to the fact that love was so individual. To Jane, it was a happiness of heart; to Aunt Gardiner, it was a comfortable companion; to Charlotte, it was security for her future. To Elizabeth, it was all these things, but more — something far deeper than those explanations had ever suggested. It was a mingling of one heart and soul with another — mixed and twisted in such a way that the two would never be separated.

Darcy watched her tilt her head, knowing she

was thinking of a reply, and, therefore, waited patiently in silence.

"Do you remember," Elizabeth began, "how you told me the first evening we were in company at Rosings, when I was playing the piano, and I was teasing you about your behaviour in Hertfordshire, that you do not have the ability to speak as easily to people as others do?"

Darcy nodded. "I do."

Elizabeth drew a breath — a deep, chest expanding breath — and then released it slowly. She knew it must be done. She must speak of her heart to him, no matter how strange it might feel. In three day's time, they would leave London and its relative peace for the loudness of Longbourn. She was uncertain if her mother would allow space for Elizabeth to draw breath, let alone contemplate and ruminate on something so important as love.

"We will find time for walks in Hertfordshire, will we not?" She could not bear the idea of quiet moments such as this being entirely removed from her. There was nothing so soothing as a stroll at Mr. Darcy's side.

"I will insist upon it." Darcy smiled down at her.

"I cannot survive without some degree of solitude. It is necessary for my well being, I assure you."

"Good," said Elizabeth, a small weight lifting from her. "You know how dearly I love a solitary walk."

"I do."

Again, she drew a breath, though not quite as great as the last one. "I do not know where to begin," she said at last. "So much has changed in such a short time." She peeked up and saw him nod his agreement. "Before you left Rosings, I had thought I might be caught up in the newness of our situation. I thought that I craved your presence because you were..." she paused as if unsure of what she was about to say.

"I was not your cousin," he supplied. Her smile at his comment caused her eyes to sparkle and his heart to flutter. "You are so beautiful," he whispered.

She ducked her head again, but her smile did not diminish. "Yes, you are sensible."

He chuckled. "I shall remind you of that when you are put out with me."

She nudged him with her shoulder. "As I was saying. I thought I craved your presence because you were sensible. I thought I enjoyed your company because you had become a friend." She peeked up at him again. "And you have become a friend, but it is more."

She stopped walking and turned to face him. She knew she must look at him while she said the words that had echoed in her mind and heart since the day her father gave her permission to marry the man in front of her. She would see his eyes as she said those words that she had questioned and contemplated. She would watch his face when she finally admitted those words that had befuddled her and had slowly drawn her into accepting their truth. "Rosings shall always have a dear place in my heart, for it is where I discovered you first in a locked bedroom," she could not resist the urge to lift a teasing brow, and he chuckled. Somehow that low rumbling sound made it easier for her to continue, "and then, in my heart. I love you," her lips curled into a smile, and her eyes glistened with happy tears, "most ardently, and I will continue to love you with my dying breath."

Darcy's lips parted and then slid into the most endearing smile Elizabeth had ever seen, for it not only curved his mouth but shone on his face and beamed from his eyes. It was joy, pure joy. "You love me?"

She nodded. "I do. I do not know how it happened or precisely when, but I love you."

Darcy gave no thought to the people who might come upon him and Elizabeth as they stood in the garden. Nor did he think about those who might be watching from the house. He did not even consider the teasing that would come from Richard about the poor example he was setting for Georgiana. He only knew that Elizabeth loved him and that such a declaration demanded he take her in his arms, which he did.

Elizabeth wrapped her arms around his neck and wove her fingers through his hair as she returned his kiss. This. This was where she wished to remain; here, with this man who loved her completely and whom she knew would always hold her heart.

Epilogue

Darcy stepped down from the carriage and extended his hand to help his wife alight before tending to his son.

"No, no, I will take him," Richard said as he tossed the reins of his horse to a groom and hurried toward the Darcys' carriage to scoop up his namesake before the child's father could claim him. Two-year-old Alexander Darcy — Alexander was Richard's middle name — squealed with delight as his uncle swept him into the air and placed him on his shoulder.

"Return him in an hour," said Elizabeth. "He will be tired and hungry and not at all pleasant if you keep him out longer than that."

"Ah, we will not be hungry, will we Alex? Uncle Richard will find you a biscuit."

"An hour." Elizabeth's tone was firm. Richard

was an excellent uncle when he was not being indulgent. She leaned on Darcy's arm and whispered, "How do you suppose he will react when we tell him that he is to be an uncle a second time?" She placed her hand on her abdomen that was only now beginning to feel full and slightly rounded.

Darcy chuckled. "Delighted. He has claimed that he wishes to see every room in Pemberley filled."

It was true. Richard had taken to the idea of being an uncle quickly and with the same fervour with which he approached most tasks. He promised that he would teach the child to ride and shoot, and he would see him well-educated at Darcy's expense.

"Then he had best find himself a wife and get on with the filling of the rooms. He is not getting any younger," Elizabeth said with a laugh.

"We will not be filling them all?" Darcy waggled his brows and smiled at his wife.

"No, we will not. We must save some room for my father, mother, and sisters when they visit."

And visit they would — often, as they already had. Darcy was becoming accustomed to the commotion Elizabeth's mother created on each and every visit, and he welcomed the times he could spend tucked away in the library with her father, for he had come to realize that though the man lacked exertion, he did not lack intellect. They had spent many a pleasurable hour in discussions of various books or locked in a strategic battle on a chess board.

Georgiana had been delighted to have ladies of about her age with whom to discuss all the topics that young ladies discuss behind bedroom doors while wearing robes and slippers and sipping tea as the candle burns low and hisses.

Elizabeth had been terrified to allow her sisters to spend unsupervised time with Georgiana. Georgiana was all that was proper. She was young, but she was calm and reserved where Elizabeth's youngest sisters were excitable and outgoing. However, Elizabeth had not taken into account the effect of thirty thousand pounds and of aunts who were ladies of the first circles with connections to titles could have on impressionable young ladies who wished to snare eligible husbands and improve their lots in life.

Apparently, with the correct incentive, even

Lydia could be found learning to play the piano while Kitty sang and Mary painted. It was remarkable, really, how the quality of the society in which her sisters now found themselves had elevated their own expectations of their behavior.

Darcy waited as Elizabeth removed her hat and pelisse. "Are you ready?" There was always an interview of sorts to endure whenever the Darcys arrived at Rosings. Lady Catherine would wish to know about their trip, as well as any news about Georgiana and the Bennet girls. Just as she did when she travelled to Pemberley or visited with Darcy in London, Lady Catherine would also demand that Alexander stand before her for inspection, upon the completion of which there was always some small treat to be had. However, today, that inspection would have to wait until Uncle Richard had had his playtime.

"I am. We should not keep her waiting."

When it came to Darcy's family, Elizabeth had found her footing quickly. Richard was a teasing elder brother. Georgiana was a loving sister. Lord and Lady Matlock were welcoming, as was their son, the Viscount and his wife. And then there were Lady Catherine and Anne. Anne was a faithful correspondent, informing Elizabeth of all that was newsworthy in Kent. Anne's mother was a doting great-aunt and regarded Elizabeth more as a daughter than a niece. She had even taken it upon herself to introduce Elizabeth — and Jane — to London's society.

That was the only place where Elizabeth's transition into her new life had been truly daunting. Lady Catherine had not been in society for many years, and so her connections were not what they once were. There were frequent arguments between Lady Catherine and her brother, Lord Matlock, about what engagements were truly important for the new Mrs. Darcy and Mrs. Bingley to attend. Whether it was because Lord Matlock knew more about society than Lady Catherine or just more about Darcy's aversion to society, Elizabeth did not care, for his interference had kept her home and afforded her time for solitude and reading.

"Did Charles not join you?" Lady Catherine said after greeting both Darcy and Elizabeth with a kiss on the cheek.

Charles Bingley had found himself taken in as a member of the family by Lady Catherine. If there was one thing that Darcy's aunt found tantalizing, it was the prospect of offering guidance — by way of instruction and reprimand — to those whom she deemed in need of such service. Bingley, being both from trade and an orphan, was, in Lady Catherine's opinion, decidedly in need of her assistance. Thankfully, Bingley was an amiable man, and his wife was longsuffering, for Lady Catherine was not always tactful in her instruction. Unfortunately, or perhaps happily for some, Caroline Ainsworth, née Bingley, was not as amiable as her brother and soon decided it was best not to be found very often in Lady Catherine's presence. Therefore, she determined to keep herself to her husband's sphere of friends as much as possible.

"We left earlier, so that we could call on the parsonage before arriving at Rosings," Darcy explained as he led Elizabeth to a sofa.

"Another?"

Darcy looked at his aunt in confusion. "Pardon me. Another what?"

"Child." She waved her hand at Elizabeth. "Your wife is walking as if she is with child. You cannot keep avoiding society in such a fashion,

Darcy." Her tone was stern, but she smiled. "I do hope it is a girl this time," she said as she took her seat. "My given name is Catherine Estella, you know."

This was not new information to either Elizabeth or Darcy. Lady Catherine had contributed a great list of acceptable names during Elizabeth's first pregnancy. "Estella is beautiful," said Elizabeth.

"Indeed," said Lady Catherine, settling back in her chair and looking satisfied that her name would one day be borne by a Darcy child.

"The child is expected to arrive before the season, and we intend to be in town with Georgiana and Elizabeth's sisters during the season," said Darcy.

Lady Catherine clucked her tongue. "Still unmarried, and so pretty." She was nearly as bad as Mrs. Bennet in wishing to see all the Bennet daughters well married. "We shall have to see what can be done on that front."

"But what of Anne?" asked Darcy. "Will she not need you here?"

"She has her husband and Mrs. Jenkinson, and I will not be far if I am needed."

Anne had married the spring following Darcy and Elizabeth's fateful trip to Rosings. Mr. Abney had indeed been interested in courting Anne, and once Darcy had stepped away, Mr. Abney had taken very little time in making his intentions known. They, their daughter, and Mrs. Jenkinson, who had been retained to help care for the child, lived at an estate ten miles from Rosings and nearer to London.

"You will not miss your grandchild too much?" Darcy teased.

"I should say not. I shall visit Anne on my trip to town and again when I return, and while I am in town, I shall have others to snuggle." She smiled at the thought. "I have had Cook make biscuits just for Alexander — his own tin."

"He and Uncle Richard will be pleased," said Elizabeth with a laugh.

Lady Catherine tipped her head and nodded slowly. "He is very good with children, is he not?"

"Surprisingly so," said Darcy. "He was never so kind to me when we were children. However, he has always been understanding and gentle with Georgiana, so, I suppose, it should not surprise me so."

"He is selling his commission." Lady Catherine straightened the hem of her sleeve.

"Does he know this?" Darcy asked.

Lady Catherine shrugged. "He has been considering the idea, but I may have helped it along."

Darcy shook his head and chuckled. His aunt had always been meddlesome, but in the last three years, she had become even more so.

She straightened the hem of her other sleeve. "It is time he marry." She looked up with a knowing grin. "And I believe I have found just the lady."

Before You Go

If you enjoyed this book, be sure to let others know by leaving a review.

~*~*~

Do you want to know when the next Leenie B book will be available?

You can when you sign up to my mailing list.

Book News from Leenie Brown

(bit.ly/LeenieBBookNews)

~*~*~

Turn the page to read an excerpt of another one of Leenie's books

Not an Heiress
Excerpt

The next book in the Dash of Darcy and Companions Collection is the sequel to the story you just read. Not an Heiress features the same scheming Lady Catherine, who is intent on seeing another Bennet daughter happily married to one of her nephews.

PROLOGUE

Mr. Bennet settled back in his chair and studied the lady who sat in front of his desk. It was not their first meeting. They had spent several hours in various conversations during his latest stay at Pemberley.

"You are still of the belief that Colonel Fitzwilliam holds a tendre for my Mary?"

Lady Catherine de Bourgh liked Mr. Bennet. He did not dance around a subject — one could be direct with the man. He was also not the sort of gentleman to dismiss a lady simply because she wore a dress and was capable of bearing children. "I am certain. My brother, Lord Matlock, informs me that his son Richard has spent the best part of the season attempting to find a wife."

"That does not signify that he holds my Mary in regard."

Lady Catherine smiled. "Perhaps, but I find it curious that each lady has been found lacking despite her beauty and fortune."

Mr. Bennet shrugged. "He has simply not found that for which he is looking. It is not so unusual."

"Mr. Bennet, I must disagree. He has found the one he needs to marry. He is just unwilling to accept her because she does not yet have a fortune." She saw Mr. Bennet's head begin to shake, but she was not about to allow him to contradict her. She had adequate proof that her supposition was correct, so she shared a sampling. "His father heard him asking one very well dowered young lady whether she read Fordyce, and when she replied in the negative, he thanked her for the dance and departed. He never approached her again."

Mr. Bennet's eyes had grown wide, and he had leaned forward eagerly interested.

"My nephew has also grumbled loudly that most of the ladies he has taken for a picnic or a drive do not consider it their place to care for the children. They would prefer a nurse or governess see to the task of raising the next generation of offspring, which you know is not unusual, but it is the opposite of how your daughter views the responsibilities of a mother."

Mr. Bennet nodded. Mary had always spoken firmly in defense of a mother's role in caring for her children. And that defense often contained a quote from the scriptures such as that bit about Timothy's mother. Mr. Bennet scratched just below his ear. He should be able to remember it as oft as he had heard it.

"Those ladies also were never approached again." Lady Catherine straightened the hem of her sleeve. "Mark my words, Mr. Bennet, my nephew was comparing them to Miss Mary and has found them wanting."

It was logic that Mr. Bennet could not deny. "So, you have devised a way to make my Mary acceptable to him?"

Lady Catherine inclined her head and gave a half shrug. "I should like him to accept her regardless of what those documents say." She pointed to the packet of papers lying before Mr. Bennet. Then with a last fidget of straightening her sleeve, she held his gaze. "However, I intend to force the issue much as I did with Darcy."

A sparkle of amusement shone in Mr. Bennet's eyes. She had hoped his wish to be amused by the folly of others might assist her in her scheme, and it appeared it would.

"I am not opposed to a compromise," he said, "as long as it is evident that both will be happy with the results."

"I could not agree more. I should not wish either unhappy, for I shall, after all, be forced to live with that happiness or lack thereof."

Mr. Bennet nodded slowly. "Then I give my permission to arrange the match however you see fit." He touched the place where he had signed the documents to ensure the ink had dried before he folded them and pushed them across the desk toward Lady Catherine. "The second son of an earl is not a bad catch for my Mary."

Lady Catherine allowed it to be so as she picked

up the papers from the desk and placed them in the bag she had brought with her. "I should very much like to have you and your family visit Rosings in one month from today."

Mr. Bennet's brows furrowed.

Lady Catherine rose. "Your wife will not be opposed to a wedding breakfast in Kent, will she?" It was such fun to see a man's eyes pop open wide and his mouth drop open. She had enjoyed creating that expression when just a girl, and it seemed the pleasure did not fade as one aged. She waited while Mary's father mentally gathered himself.

"I should think she will be delighted," Mr. Bennet finally managed to reply.

"The earl and countess will also be in attendance." Her lips pursed as she struggled to keep a grin in check. "I would advise you to bring whatever documents are needed for all to be settled quickly. I shall see that a license is secured." She extended her hand to Mr. Bennet. "I do so like doing business with a man who knows how to come to the point quickly."

Mr. Bennet gave her hand a firm shake to seal

their deal. "You will ensure she is happy?" he asked, still holding Lady Catherine's hand.

She nodded. Lady Catherine could understand his hesitance. Parents of any true worth always worried for the happiness of their children. "I would not accept any less than pure delight." She smiled as he lifted her hand and kissed it. "I shall see you in one month?"

"One month," he assured her.

She moved to exit the room but then stopped just short of the door. "You will not mention the need for the visit, will you? I should hate for the surprise to be ruined for Miss Mary." Indeed, her plans would likely come to naught if word reached Mary before they could be put into action.

"Not a word until three weeks hence." He chuckled. "I can only endure the raptures of my wife in minuscule amounts, and the mere thought of being invited to an estate such as Rosings and being in the presence of a real lady will send her soaring."

Lady Catherine chuckled as she reached for the door handle. She had witnessed some of Mrs. Bennet's raptures over the past three years, and she did not envy Mr. Bennet's place in having to endure them as often as she suspected he did. "You are a wise man, Mr. Bennet." She pulled the door open. "One month," she repeated and waited to get a nod of acceptance before exiting his study.

Acknowledgements

As with all of my books, there are many who have had a part in the creation of this story. Some have read and commented on it. Some have proofread for grammatical errors and plot holes. Others have not even read the story (and a few, I know, will never read it), but their encouragement and belief in my ability, as well as their patience when I became cranky or when supper was late or the groceries ran low, was invaluable.

And so, I would like to thank Zoe, Rose, Betty, Kristine, Ben, and Kyle, as well as the lovely readers in my private Facebook group, Leenie's Sweeties, who read an advance copy of the story and helped me create both the epilogue and sequel to this book.

I have not listed my dear husband in the above group because, to me, he deserves his own special thank you, for without his somewhat pushy insistence that I start sharing my writing, none of my writing goals and dreams would have been met.

Other Leenie B Books

You can find all of Leenie's books at this link
bit.ly/LeenieBBooks
where you can explore the collections below

~*~

Other Pens, Mansfield Park

~*~

Touches of Austen Collection

~*~

Other Pens, Pride and Prejudice

~*~

Dash of Darcy and Companions Collection

~*~

Marrying Elizabeth Series

~*~

Willow Hall Romances

~*~

The Choices Series

~*~

Darcy Family Holidays

~*~

Darcy and... An Austen-Inspired Collection

About the Author

Leenie Brown has always been a girl with an active imagination, which, while growing up, was both an asset, providing many hours of fun as she played out stories, and a liability, when her older sister and aunt would tell her frightening tales. At one time, they had her convinced Dracula lived in the trunk at the end of the bed she slept in when visiting her grandparents!

Although it has been years since she cowered in her bed in her grandparents' basement, she still has an imagination which occasionally runs away with her, and she feeds it now as she did then — by reading!

Her heroes, when growing up, were authors, and the worlds they painted with words were (and still are) her favourite playgrounds! Now, as an adult, she spends much of her time in the Regency world, playing with the characters from her favourite Jane Austen novels and those of her own creation.

When she is not traipsing down a trail in an attempt to keep up with her imagination, Leenie resides in the beautiful province of Nova Scotia with her two sons and her very own Mr. Brown (a wonderful mix of all the best of Darcy, Bingley, and Edmund with a healthy dose of the teasing Mr. Tilney and just a dash of the scolding Mr. Knightley).

Connect with Leenie Brown

E-mail:
LeenieBrownAuthor@gmail.com
Facebook:
www.facebook.com/LeenieBrownAuthor
Blog:
leeniebrown.com
Patreon:
https://www.patreon.com/LeenieBrown
Subscribe to Leenie's Mailing List:
Book News from Leenie Brown
(bit.ly/LeenieBBookNews)

Made in the USA
Lexington, KY
21 August 2019